For Paul

Diversion Books
A Division of Diversion Publishing Corp.
443 Park Avenue South, Suite 1004
New York, New York 10016
www.DiversionBooks.com

For more information, email info@diversionbooks.com

First Diversion Books edition May 2014.

Print ISBN: 978-1-62681-301-4
eBook ISBN: 978-1-62681-294-9

as is

rachel michael arends

DIVERSIONBOOKS

chapter one

gwendolyn

I rarely pass through a room without running into someone measuring something, or moving something, or setting up or taking down something. I have lived and worked in this mansion for four years. In the beginning it was quiet, sometimes even peaceful. But now that it's known as the *So Perfect* house, this place feels about as calm and real as a circus.

I am the face of *So Perfect*. That means I often have to be prepped for a video blog or television segment, or have my hair and makeup done for a photo shoot, or cook for the cameras. Or I may have to pose, sew, entertain, schmooze, upholster, or any other of a number of tricks the lion tamers crack their whips and tell me to perform. On television it can look glamorous, and perhaps some people would love this lifestyle. But I don't. Whenever I can, I escape to my attic art studio; it's off limits to everyone but me, and sometimes my partner, Armand. I don't think I would have survived this long without it.

"Time to clean in here now, Miss G."

I look up to see Alejandra enter my bedroom. Though I'm in my pajamas, I'm not startled by her sudden appearance. People come and go all the time around here. Sometimes even my bed is photographed if pillows or throws are going into the next *So Perfect* catalog. Not even my bed is really my own. Nothing is.

"Are you excited for your trip?" I ask. Alejandra and her husband Miguel rarely take any time off. They plan to go out of town to visit relatives for a long weekend and I'm happy for them. I'm happy for me, too; the whole house will be clearing out and I'll finally get to spend some time alone.

"Yes! My sisters are planning a big party," she says as she tidies the room.

I take a bag of wrapped presents from the closet and give it to her. "I finished those little paintings for your nieces," I say.

"Oh, they will love them, Miss G.!" She hugs me tight. "Now hurry or Mr. Armand will be so mad."

"Good morning!" Armand says, smiling wide when I enter the kitchen. He always manages to look amazing, and he never fidgets with his clothes or seems to get tired of the limelight. It's as if he actually enjoys being *So Perfect* all the time. He sent the hair and makeup people into my room because I was running late. They did the best they could with their few minutes, but I can tell Armand isn't quite satisfied.

The kitchen is already full of people and cameras.

"Hi," I say, waving to everyone. It's embarrassing to meet fans because I know full well I don't deserve their adulation. Whenever I see my photographs in the *So Perfect* catalog, it just seems wrong, incongruous, and unnatural. Like putting stilettos on George Clooney, or casting Miley Cyrus as a nun, or telling Matt Damon to hide his twenty-million-dollar smile. When I see myself making risotto or a key lime pie on television I can't believe people buy it. The trouble is, they do. They really do. And I'm contractually obligated to keep right on selling.

Armand glides over and pecks me on the cheek. "Wrong shoes," he whispers.

I pretend I don't hear. The pointy toe pumps he left out with today's clothes pinched too much so I gave them to Lily, the gardener. She happened to be working in the antique rose garden outside the window and she wears my shoe size.

"Hello there, Gwendolyn," Stuart Bolder says, air kissing me. He's the reporter for the local station, WJKS, who hosts our weekly lifestyle segments that are edited to make me look like a pro. "Anyone who wants to, come on up and shake hands with Gwendolyn before we get started. She won't bite!" he says.

I shake hands with the people who file up. I smile at each of them warmly because it's not their fault I don't want to be here.

Today we're doing a kitchen segment, which means there isn't enough room for a full live audience. Armand can fit fifty people on folding benches in the dining room for a decorating or entertaining piece, but only a handful in here. Though he likes to complain about its limitations, I know Armand adores this house.

"Are you looking forward to your weekend alone here?" he asks when I join him at the granite island where little glass bowls of ingredients are impeccably arranged.

"Nah. I changed my mind. I'm joining you in the Big Apple instead," I tease, putting my hand lightly around his waist in our trademark stance.

He shakes his head slyly. "Not on your life."

Armand has made himself at home in this historic southern town along the Cape Fear River where tours are conducted by horse and carriage over cobblestoned streets. He walks around like he's the Lord Mayor, hamming for photographs, and chatting with anyone who recognizes him. He clearly loves it. But I know he's also anxious to disappear into an anonymous city for a few days.

Armand and I stand in our places for a lighting check and to review the script. We're making seafood omelets this morning. We went over it all yesterday. Armand smiles confidently for the cameras; he's an absolute natural. He should have been at the center of the *So Perfect* stage. That's what we both signed up for.

I'm the opposite of my partner. I find it scary and unnerving when strangers approach me as if we're old friends. I don't like to worry about what I wear, if my hair and makeup look good enough (according to Armand they never do), what I say, or how I say it. I prefer to stay at home behind our high fences, inside our security system. Whenever I can, I sneak up to the attic and lose myself in a painting.

Trey Hammond, President of *So Perfect*, appears out of nowhere. He's taller than I am even when I wear heels. He has a crazy amount of self-confidence, which I used to find incredibly appealing.

"Can we talk after the taping?" I ask.

"Absolutely," he says. But I know from experience that he'll try to leave before I can say a word. I want to discuss my contract. I have been attempting to negotiate my way out of the company since our first catalog launched. Originally Trey hired me for a very limited role, but he has since expanded what's expected of me. He has said on more than one occasion that I'm lucky to have this job, that anyone in her right mind would want it.

I would simply walk away and face whatever consequences Trey doled out if it were only my life on the line. I've had Armand to think of from the beginning, though. Alejandra and Miguel joined us soon after, and now there's Lily, and many more good people who depend on *So Perfect*. I don't want to let anyone down.

"We should do an anniversary portrait," Trey says, picking up a small, framed wedding photo of Armand and me from a side table.

"That sounds fun! Right, Gwendolyn?" Armand puts his arm around my shoulder and gives it a squeeze. I try to smile but only manage a wince.

The idea of a lifestyle guru couple wasn't the original premise of *So Perfect*, but it came along soon after I was hired to do original art for our product line and to appear in the catalog. Armand and I apparently had great photographic chemistry, and we certainly had a good time together. Trey pitched the idea for us to pose as a married couple in the debut catalog: setting a table for a dinner party, making dessert, having a glass of wine on the patio… whatever showed our wares to their best advantage. That catalog turned into an unexpectedly big hit. We were asked to do some interviews about our products, and Trey said that because everybody assumed we were married we should just play along. I didn't like the idea, and Armand didn't either, but Trey talked us into it. I know it sounds insane now, seeing how huge the lie has become, but back then it didn't seem so bad. It honestly didn't.

Trey winks at us and puts the photograph back on the table.

It's mortifying to remember the day that damn picture was taken. Armand had chosen an outfit for me consisting of a pencil skirt, white silk blouse, and heels that still kept me shorter than him, always important. Trey had suggested that Armand put me in a wedding dress for the portrait, but I refused. I feared it might jinx me from ever getting to wear one legitimately.

Later I found out that Armand sent a copy of the photograph to his mother, and he actually pretended to her that we'd gotten married. It was the first real red flag that I was in way over my head, that our marriage of convenience was a surreal cover story for Armand on more levels than one.

"Are we ready to roll?" Armand asks.

We get right down to business. Armand sits on a stool at the granite island, playing his role of adoring husband while I make an omelet for the cameras. I describe each step along the way, smiling and trying my best to seem competent. Stuart asks casual questions and the three of us banter. Armand gently corrects me when I do something wrong, like overheating the pan or adding ingredients in the wrong order. We get through it. Stuart eats the omelet like it's the best thing he has ever tasted, as usual.

Trey slips out a side door just as taping wraps, and Stuart's producer won't let me run after him since I'm still tethered to their microphone. I'm beginning to fear that I'll be trapped in this mansion forever.

"What are you going to do with yourself this weekend?" Armand asks while we make our way from the kitchen after bidding adieu to the staff and audience.

"I'm going to paint," I say.

"Duh. But won't you be lonely?" he asks.

I used to live by myself in an apartment over a small gallery. I worked and slept in one room while I tried to make it as a painter. It was a very, very quiet life. Occasionally whole days passed when I didn't use my voice at all, when I didn't see another living being, when I wasn't seen. It was a small white space with a tall ceiling, filled nearly to the brim with canvases in various states of completion. Sometimes I miss it so much I could cry.

This weekend will be the first time in over a year that I'll be here alone. I can't wait to experience the peace, the quiet, and the soul-replenishing work made possible by seventy-two hours of uninterrupted studio time.

"Want to watch an episode of *House Hunters International* before I catch my flight?" Armand asks.

"Are you luring me to the TV to critique my performance today?"

"Oh no, there's not nearly enough time for that!" He laughs and points to my bedroom door. "Change out of your nice things and put on one of your scary Cinderella *before* ensembles. I'll meet you at the TV in twenty minutes with a batch of caramel corn."

Caramel corn is my favorite.

Cozying up together on the sofa, Armand and I watch two episodes of his favorite show and finish off the popcorn. Then he takes me up to his room and tries on several outfits he plans to wear in the city. Armand looks good in anything and he knows it. He still likes to hear me say it, though. So I do.

The house grows quieter and quieter throughout the day as people depart for the long weekend. When Alejandra and Miguel are the last ones left Alejandra hugs me very tightly. "Don't forget to eat," she says.

"I won't," I tell her. I wave as I watch the door close behind them.

I wake with the birds and climb the stairs to the attic. I plan to commune with my canvases for three days straight, breaking only to eat and sleep.

I think I might hear the doorbell ring around eight, but when I pause for a moment with my brush in the air I don't hear it again. I figure it's my imagination because Miguel said he'd lock the gates when they left last night. I never answer the door anyway.

At nine-thirty I head down the wide, wooden staircase to make a pot of coffee. On the landing halfway to the foyer I look out the window and freeze.

There's a television news van parked out front, with WJKS emblazoned on the side. Stuart Bolder is standing on the lawn. He's wearing a black wool overcoat and red scarf on this overcast January morning. He's talking to a cameraman a few feet in front of him.

I duck into the living room and try to think. Nothing is scheduled today. If there were, I wouldn't be alone here; twenty other people would be milling around. Something about the situation feels very wrong—even more than usual. I notice a few tourists gathered at the wrought iron fence, looking in. I quickly close the plantation shutters on the floor-to-ceiling windows.

I turn on the TV and tune to WJKS.

I see a live video feed of the front of this house, with the words *SO PERFECT SCANDAL* scrolling underneath in red letters. The remote shakes in my hand and I drop it onto the sofa.

Stuart fills the frame. He raises his eyebrows and shakes his head, as if he's personally outraged. "A few hours ago this story looked like a simple yet salacious case of adultery: Armand Leopold was caught cheating on his wife and business partner, Gwendolyn Golden." Stuart holds up a newspaper with a photo of Armand passionately kissing someone.

Oh my *God*.

Armand usually wears a disguise if he's going out: a cap over his short brown hair, some stylish dark glasses to cover his striking gray eyes. In the photo he's exposed, right down to his tongue.

"But our trusty WJKS investigative reporter, Shelley Simon, has done some digging." Stuart motions his thumb toward the house like a hitchhiker. "For the past four years, Gwendolyn Golden and Armand Leopold have lived here, in what everyone refers to as the *So Perfect* mansion. The supposedly happily married couple's *So Perfect* catalog, as well as their television cooking and decorating spots, prominently feature this restored beauty on Third Street here in Scenic, North Carolina."

Stuart frowns severely, apparently reminding everyone that although he might have chatted with Armand and me on air yesterday, and he may even have complimented our omelet, today we are not his friends.

"We here in Scenic embraced Gwendolyn Golden and Armand Leopold as our own. The 'happy couple' lived among us, dined, shopped. They influenced our meals and our homes. Our children recognized them, perhaps asked them for autographs. Occasionally the couple invited tourists and locals inside this house to make a live audience. I personally have interviewed them many times, and I was just as fooled as you." He shakes his head like he's torn between crying and lighting a torch to set the house on fire. "As WJKS exclusively reports this morning, *So Perfect* is a scam. From the marriage, right on down to the talent, it has all been lies, lies, lies."

Stuart has thanked Armand and me several times for helping to make his career. Due to our popularity, he said, he has landed several guest spots on national shows. I consider going out and reasoning with him, pleading our case in a civilized way. I mean, it's not as if I've got hostages in here!

I probably shouldn't be seen LIVE in my pink flannel pajama pants and old *Friends* t-shirt, though, with my hair piled high in an ancient scrunchy. Armand would have a fit if I were photographed this way, especially today, when our downfall is suddenly broadcast live. I notice aquamarine paint on the remote and furiously wipe it with my shirt hem.

Stuart recaps the story for viewers tuning in. "*So Perfect?* WJKS's Shelley Simon has confirmed that Gwendolyn Golden and Armand Leopold have never been married. According to exclusive interviews with their housekeepers this morning, WJKS has discovered that the pretend marriage was only the quicksand foundation for their house of lies."

Most of the staff members who work on site believe that Armand and I really are the *So Perfect* couple. Granted, I'm sure they think we oversell ourselves in several ways. We can't hide the fact that I'm hopeless in the kitchen, have to be prompted at every step in the cooking segments, and mispronounce even the most rudimentary French terms. I'm similarly decorating disabled and couldn't accessorize a room to save my life. Armand

and I have separate bedroom suites; I say that he has sleep apnea and snores like a chainsaw, and he probably says the same thing about me. Trey has made the few people who know the whole truth sign confidentiality agreements.

Including Alejandra and Miguel.

I can still smell the cinnamon rolls that Alejandra baked before she left last night. "So you don't starve, Miss G. You're too thin," Alejandra had wrapped the cinnamon rolls individually, and told me to put one in the microwave for twenty seconds when I wanted a treat.

I wonder how the WJKS reporter got Alejandra and Miguel to talk. I feel protective of them, and I know they wouldn't hurt me on purpose. During the past four years I've spent more time with them than anyone except Armand. They're more like family to me than my family.

I feel woozy at the realization that people watching won't know what's real and what's not. I feel woozier as it sinks in that I'm probably the last person in the world who should complain about that today.

I turn off the television; I don't want to see any more. I press a button and the large, flat screen above the ornate fireplace is hidden by red Chinese doors that slide into place.

Armand designed it, like everything else in this restored mansion he calls the Grand Dame. The first time I met him he said he even had a vision for a "signature Gwendolyn Golden style." Apparently it didn't strike him as odd that the signature on me would be his.

I try his cell. Armand is the only person who can possibly relate to what I'm experiencing, to the fears marching through my mind, to the voice in my head saying we brought this on ourselves.

His phone is turned off.

I rack my brain, but besides Armand, I don't really have anyone to call. Once you're famous locally you may as well be Lady Gaga because everywhere you go people point and stare. It's not exactly conducive to starting casual friendships, and dating is impossible when you're supposedly happily married.

Even among those who work for *So Perfect*, I've had to be wary to uphold the confidentiality clauses in my contract. I put down my phone and sigh, realizing that I've waried myself down to no one.

My phone rings and I see a name that promises to round out one of the worst mornings I've ever had. My sister Megan has always been oil in my water, hair on my toothbrush, onions in my milkshake. At least I can be glad that she's not in Scenic to witness the local scandal.

"Good morning, Megan."

"Is it?" she snaps.

"Isn't it?" I ask, wishing I sounded tougher. I notice a smear of aquamarine paint on the distressed leather sofa and break out in a cold sweat.

"I'm taking Dad to the hospital." Megan's tone implies that it's my fault.

"What's wrong?" I ask, closing my eyes tight and hoping it's something small. He dropped a can of soup on his foot. He cut his finger. *Not his heart again. Don't let it be his heart.*

"Let's see… Oh, that's right. His heart palpitations began when he saw you on the news."

"I'm on the news there, too?" So it is my fault.

"Yes. Isn't that lovely? My colleagues, Dad's friends, my kids' teachers, in short, *everyone* can see your filthy laundry aired on television."

"Is Dad okay?" I ask.

"He was in a complete panic when he called me. Apparently he never minded that you were a fake until everyone else found out! He screamed himself blue and now he's slumped in his chair like a petulant child. I called his cardiologist and he's going to meet us at the hospital," she whispers quickly, and I imagine her with her shoulders hunched, turned away from my dad.

"Let me talk to him."

"No. You aren't going to get off with a few words on the phone, Gwen! Not this time. You have to get your ass down here! I booked you a flight that leaves at noon. You need to take some responsibility for this mess!"

"Gwennie?" It's my dad on the line. He sounds horrible. Weak. "Come on home and see your old man."

I fill an overnight bag first, then change my mind and pack a big suitcase. I'm not sure how long I'll need to be away. I don't have time for a proper shower so I toss on some clothes, wash my face, and put on ChapStick and sunscreen. I rip out my scrunchy, along with several long, wavy hairs that had wound themselves around it.

I haul my suitcase toward the garage. In the kitchen I pause to write a note about where I'm going, but I don't know whom to address. I think of Alejandra and Miguel and hope they're not in trouble with Trey for telling the truth. I think of Armand, hiding out from the scandal somewhere in New York City.

I think of my Dad and how he asked me to come home. I haven't thought of Riveredge, Michigan that way in ten years.

I check the time. That's it, I've got to leave right now or I'll miss my flight. I dread having to pass the cameraman on my way out, and I certainly don't want to see Megan when I get there. I hate my sister sometimes! Especially when she tells me that I'm a screw up.

Especially when she's right.

chapter two

armand

My mama always says that liquor is the devil himself. She says everything with a swaggering religious zeal, and if it's still not enough to convince you, she backs it up with two hundred plus pounds of whoop-ass. At thirty-one years old I'm still as afraid of her as I ever was.

Because I barely ever allow myself to enjoy a nice strong cocktail, I'm not used to hangovers. Lucky for me, my head pounds less as my shower goes on, and on, and on this morning. I love hotel showers because you never run out of hot water.

I don't recall all the details of last night, but enough comes back to me so that I'm smiling by the time I turn off the faucet. And lo and behold, when I open the curtain, Norman is standing there. He's taller than my six feet, and he's got a shaved head, brown eyes, and a body so ripped he's got muscles on his muscles. He has the kind of smile that could sell just about anything—it wouldn't matter if you needed it or not because you'd want it so bad. He hands me a cup of coffee as I step out and I think *I could get used to this.* I don't believe that I've ever seen a man so handsome.

"It's a shame it's a slow news day," he says.

I wonder what in heaven the expression on his face means. He looks like he either just heard a good joke or he has a big surprise in store. I can't decide which it is; maybe it's both. I sip coffee while I watch him. It's dark and strong, just like Norman. "Slow news day?"

"It sure is," Norman says.

He leads the way out of the bathroom. I follow behind, trying harder to recall the details of last night. I stop when Norman points to the TV.

"Your wife is attempting to pull out of your garage, but the television van is blocking her. They're showing it live." He turns back to me, grinning.

I close my eyes and rattle off a silent *Our Father* before I ask, "Why?"

"This might explain it." Norman picks up a newspaper from the nightstand and offers me the Entertainment page.

Oh Lord. There I am kissing Norman!

We're standing outside the nightclub waiting for a cab, a few hours after we'd met.

Normally I go by the name Sebastian when I'm stepping out, and I always wear one of my disguises. I'm never recognized unless I want to be. I wonder how in God's name this happened!

More memories of last night come back. It was dark in the club, and I'd had three naughtily-named drinks by the time I met Norman. He wanted to see my eyes better so I took off my sunglasses. He wanted to see my new haircut so I took off my cap. I guess someone recognized me from *So Perfect*, someone who was well connected enough to put my picture in the paper. I can't believe that we're on the news, too!

I sit down hard in an overstuffed chair and wonder if there is any way possible to keep this news from reaching my mother. I hear a siren outside and imagine her speeding right up here in an avenging Saviormobile, bent on whisking me off for a stint in homo detox.

I'd feel bad for Norman getting caught up in this mess if he weren't staring at the television like he just won a jackpot. I turn back to the paper and wince at the headline: SO PERFECT?

"I'm sorry, kid," I say to the screen.

Gwendolyn maneuvers the black Lexus SUV I picked out for her past a news van and a little crowd. She hasn't brushed her hair, she's wearing a very ugly beige t-shirt under a ratty sweater I thought I'd thrown away months ago, and she's bawling her head off. Her eyes get weirdly huge when she's upset, like a slow loris. Now she's all eyes and stringy hair on national TV. And it's all my fault.

"Bad luck, huh?" Norman asks, sounding pleased as Punch about it. He doesn't take his eyes from the screen. "You should have told me who you are! I had to read all about the real you in the paper. At least we look great."

My hangover has returned like a guilty conscience, and I feel clammy and sick to my stomach. I round up all my things and put them in the bathroom. "Will you please get out of here?" I ask Norman before locking myself inside, too.

Norman coaxes and pleads on the other side of the door. "You're transferring your anger, *Armand Leopold*. You know I could be angry with you for putting me in this situation, but I'm not. I'm happy to walk right out of here with you, arm in arm."

I run the water so I don't have to listen. Norman is the least of my worries, though. I'm outed on a grand scale, I made my best friend cry her slow loris eyes out on television, and my mother is going to blow her stack.

"Come on out, Armand! I like you, and we had fun last night. I don't mind a little limelight, either."

"You just want to use me!" I yell, though I told myself not to say anything at all, just to wait him out.

"You really want to claim the moral high ground this morning?" Norman laughs. "The way I see it, we're both opportunists, plain and simple."

That hits me like a sucker punch.

I had grabbed the chance to be the creative force behind *So Perfect* with both hands. I guess the only thing I inherited from my mother was some of her swagger, because I talked to the investors like together we were gonna conquer the world. I hadn't *really* known what was possible, but I talked like I did. I don't think the head honcho Trey Hammond had glimpsed the full potential in the beginning either, but I could tell he liked ambition. He had it too, and our ambitions lined up.

He had brought me on to make a home decorating catalog that would include cookware and recipes. I don't recall Trey's name for it, but whatever it was, it was all wrong. I had liked *So*

Perfect and got my way. I also talked Trey into letting me renovate an old southern belle of a house I'd had my eye on. It would be our headquarters, and provide a fabulous backdrop that would show our products to their full advantage.

I soon found out that Trey couldn't go up, down, or turn around without first consulting a blessed focus group. I wish I had thrown my head back and howled the first time I heard the idea, but that would've only gotten me kicked out right at the beginning. I wanted the job bad enough to listen to feedback, even though it was sometimes just about as pleasant as swallowing Brussels sprouts whole.

Trey and his opinionated groups had decided we needed a woman on board to pose with our products and personalize the company, someone accessible and non-judgmental, that our demographic would relate to. She had to be attractive, but not in a standoffish way, had to seem confident but not cold, had to do this while not doing that... the list went on and on and it gave me a headache. I suggested some former decorating pals and even paged through modeling agency and aspiring actress photos. I did these things, though I thought the idea that we needed a woman on board was downright silly.

I heft up my suitcase and set it on the long vanity. I take out my carefully folded new jeans and my heavenly soft favorite sweater and put them on. Mirrors don't lie, and this one's saying that it's sort of a crime I won't be seen out and about in NYC today. I think of poor Gwendolyn again and shake my head.

By the time Trey discovered her, I had either designed or chosen every product and recipe for *So Perfect*. I had overseen the jigsaw puzzle of the headquarters house, making sure the right pieces were taken apart and put back together correctly, while others were simply polished up and fitted into place. And though I admittedly don't tan well, my hair recedes a fraction of an inch every year, and my thighs are too big for most jeans that I love, I knew I looked good enough to pose with my products without a woman in the picture.

But that wasn't the point. The focus groups had wanted a woman, and Trey found Gwendolyn.

I agreed she looked great with the right makeup and wardrobe—certainly not left to her own devices like today. The focus groups loved Gwendolyn. Too much, actually, because it turned out they loved her far more than they loved me.

When I was told I'd have to be more of a behind-the-scenes guy, I was so crushed I had me a full bottle of the devil. I soon sobered up and knew it was still the best gig I'd ever had. It beat wedding planning, interior decorating, landscape design, and running a restaurant—all jobs I'd had, but had grown bored with after a few years.

That was all before I knew I'd have to pretend to be married, mind you. If I had known what was in store from the beginning, maybe I would have done a perfect military about-face and marched away without looking back. But who am I kidding? Once I'd had a taste of *So Perfect* I couldn't leave until I'd eaten the whole buffet.

"Are you still in there?" Norman calls.

I sit on the closed toilet seat, all dress up with nowhere to go. "No!" I shout.

Trey had picked Gwendolyn for *So Perfect* like he was giving her a grand prize, but she didn't just sign on the bottom line when he waved his checkbook. She worried about having to pretend to be someone she wasn't, so Trey gave her examples of marketing campaigns that had been built around spokespeople. He said it was a "perfectly valid marketing approach." Plenty of catalogs and websites personify their products, he said, and this was nothing new. Our Gwendolyn, though, she wasn't sold right away.

Trey took it as a challenge to sign up Gwendolyn. I don't think he'd been told "no" much in his life. When swaying her with money didn't work, he found her Achilles heel—her art. As soon as Trey discovered that Gwendolyn's lifelong dream was to become a self-supporting artist, he changed his strategy and courted her to create art for the *So Perfect* brand, and still pose for the catalog, of course. Then it was easy as pie!

Believing that she was wanted for her artistic talent made Gwendolyn feel validated as a painter. Her identity as an artist was so tied up in her identity as a person, I think she just felt validated period. Before we found her, Gwendolyn sort of lived in her own little world, with paintbrushes for friends, and canvases to talk to. I thought of her as a tragic fairy princess we were leading to her happily ever after.

Gwendolyn believed her role with *So Perfect* was a quality judgment on her work, not her looks and manner, not what the focus groups perceived as her easygoing style. I feel bad now, thinking back to how naïve Gwen was.

Is.

Probably the same reason Trey couldn't understand the word "no," because he'd never been taught it, Gwendolyn hadn't learned to fret about where her next rent payment would come from, because her daddy always helped when she was short.

This line of thinking makes me so nervous; I feel like I'm back in the broom closet at school with Lenny Nelson, and we hear the football team coming up the hall. I don't like to spend much time thinking about why people are the way they are… it hits a little too close to home. And then I start wondering, what if I had asked myself which of the things my mama said were true and which were nonsense a good long time ago? Maybe I wouldn't have been so willing to pretend to be someone I'm not. Maybe I wouldn't be the latest bloomer on the planet, hiding out from the world in a hotel bathroom.

Norman has finally gone. I tuck the phone number he left lying on the table into my pocket, just in case.

There's no sign of my story on the television any more. I'm shocked it got network coverage at all. While our catalog is now well known across the country, I wouldn't consider us national celebrities. We sometimes do segments that air on syndicated shows, but none of them have high ratings. It must be like Norman said, a slow news day, and we just caught someone's attention. I don't know what hits and what doesn't. If I did, I'd have made myself known on the world stage long before now, and I wouldn't have dragged my friend Gwendolyn down to do it.

I wonder where she was headed. The kid barely ever leaves the house without me or one of the staff. Some fairy tale we put her in—she's been locked in an ivy-covered tower.

I'd like to turn my mama on Stuart Bolder for walking on my grass, and I want to know who in God's name let him through the front gate! Maybe he snuck in the side that has a fussy latch? I wouldn't put it past him to climb over the fence.

The Grand Dame near the Cape Fear River was the first house where I actually felt at home. She wasn't perfect when I fell in love with her, but maybe that's partly why I was head over heels. I saw every botched restoration effort and cut corner as an opportunity to take her back to how she used to be, before her owners changed her, as if she hadn't been perfect to begin with. I didn't want to make her fit into a mold. I wanted her to be herself.

The hotel telephone rings. It's the concierge. "Good morning, Mr. Leopold." He has a British accent and sounds like a butler forced to take care of stinky business that's really beneath him. "I'm calling to inform you that a gaggle of reporters are flocked outside the door like nuisance pigeons. When you're ready to go, we'll escort you out a back way and have a taxi waiting."

"Oh. Thanks," I say.

"Will you be leaving soon, sir?" he prompts.

"I don't know."

"Very well then." He sounds extremely disappointed. "Simply call down when you've made up your mind."

I gather up all my things and notice that my cell phone has been off. I turn it on to find that I've missed twenty calls. Ten from Trey—no surprise there—he likes to give my *So Perfect* leash a good hard yank every time I misstep. Two calls from Gwendolyn, the poor kid. And I don't know the other numbers, except one. Seeing my mama's name on my list of missed calls, I feel like ducking for cover.

chapter three

smith

Taylor enters my office quickly and quietly, stirring the closed-in air like a healthy breeze. I can't remember if I always appreciated the grace with which he moves, or if it's only in contrast to how cumbersome and uncooperative my own body has become. He places a neat stack of mail on the corner of my wide oak desk and pats the newspaper on top, which has already been taken out of its bag and folded over once.

My youngest brother is conscientious, careful, and very smart. The fact that Taylor looks up to me almost like a father—a role I've been playing since our dad died when he was thirteen—might make me a bit biased. I admit that. But everyone who meets Taylor seems to agree with my assessment that he's pretty special.

I wish fewer people compared us to each other, though. They always describe me in past tense when they do: *Taylor is just as tall and skinny as you used to be. Taylor loves exercise and the outdoors, just like you did. Taylor always gets the prettiest girls, just like you used to.* But I can't blame him for being like me in better days, even if the comparisons make me wince.

Taylor is my right-hand man. I wish I could claim that all my other forays into nepotism have paid off equally well, but I'd be lying and I hate to lie. The two truthful things I can say about everyone on my growing payroll are: one, they're all very nice people, and two, they need bread on their tables. In this economy where getting ahead means swimming upstream and over rapids—with no guarantee of better prospects even if you manage to get to the top—I find myself hiring out jobs that would be a whole lot easier to leave undone.

I realize I should be used to too much responsibility; it has defined my life, after all. But now that I have a more acute sense of my own mortality, I'm torn. On one hand, I wish fewer folks depended on me for their livelihoods. On the other, I rack my brain trying to think of more things to hire out so that I can write checks. The sad truth is that this recession has knocked too many good people on their asses, and I know it's important for a person to work for his living, important to the heart and self-respect. I remind everyone to be aware of their options, though, and to keep looking out for something better. "After all, I could get hit by a truck tomorrow," I say. No one really likes that joke.

Taylor gives me a knowing glance. Sometimes I still think of him as a kid, but then he'll shoot me a look like this that reminds me he's all grown up. He's no longer the only Walker boy who cried in front of people when he got hurt, or sang to his mom every time she asked to hear him, or even the skinny electrical engineering grad who couldn't find a job close to home and therefore came to me, hat in hand, two years ago.

I remember wanting out of town so badly when I younger; I couldn't quite believe that Taylor didn't seize the chance to run. I had to stay because my dad died young, and our family was so poor I had no choice but to work to support my mom and four younger brothers. I attended college on an academic scholarship and still graduated on time, thanks to understanding professors, a flexible boss, and my own work ethic. Taylor was the crying, singing baby of the family, who has somehow become a man. I only offered him work on the condition that he keep searching for a job in his field, but he shows every intention of staying right here. When I complain that he should move on already, he says it's my fault because I pay him more than his friends who landed engineering jobs and got the hell out of Michigan.

"What's on your mind, Taylor?" I ask.

His look says I should know. My replying look says that I don't know, and he should get on with telling me before I lose my patience.

"I'll be back here at ten-thirty so we can make it to the 404 building by eleven. Meanwhile, you might be interested in today's newspaper," he says.

Our eleven o'clock meeting is a big one. Commercial real estate in Michigan isn't exactly what you'd call a hot field at the moment, and by "moment" I mean the past several years and likely the next several. If we get the contracts signed today, we'll have made our biggest deal in the past two years, and it will carry my growing payroll for a good little while. As business has slowed, I haven't been all that worried about myself. Personally, I've not only been careful, but I've also been lucky with my investments and holdings. I worry more about the people who look to me for their bread. Taylor is out the door before I can ask him a few more questions about the big meeting. I know we're ready, though, so I pick up the newspaper.

"What's the matter, Smith?" Jessie calls in alarm from the outer office. She's the mousiest and most hovering secretary I can even imagine. While I value Taylor and would be lost without him, I think I might throw a party if Jessie quits. She is married to my cousin Jack, who has never held a job, in good times or in bad. I hired Jessie when my mom told me how poor they were and asked if I could find something for one of them. I figured dealing with Jessie was better than Jack, and I hate to say no to my mom.

"Why, Jessie?" I ask, very slowly. I always speak to her slowly because her brain operates like a stick shift being driven by a teenage girl. I have to give Jessie time to lurch and fall back a few times before she catches on.

"You made a sound like you were surprised."

"Well, I was!"

"Are you okay?"

"Yes, Jessie. I'm okay," I say, closing the conversation.

I caught my breath when I looked at the paper, and apparently I can't catch my breath without Jessie thinking I'm going to keel over dead. It wasn't the face in the photo that surprised me; I know that face better than I know my own, even if I don't see it in the paper every day. It was the below-the-fold headline: LOCAL STAR IN SCANDAL.

I'm only halfway through reading the article when Shirley the cleaner comes in. She drops her supply bucket, puts her hands on her hips, and demands, "What are you doing here, Smith Walker? I always clean this place on Friday mornings!"

"Just go ahead and skip my office," I tell her. I'm annoyed at being interrupted, and at her tone. Typically I'm not here on Friday mornings because I'm at the hospital seeing Irene, but I had to switch out today for the big meeting.

Shirley barrels in and empties my trash as if I hadn't said a word. She points to the paper. "That woman ought to be ashamed of herself."

"Skip my office," I tell Shirley again, firmly enough this time so that she picks up her bucket and waddles out in a huff.

"Please close the damn door," I call. She slams it.

I look at Gwen's photograph again, though I don't need it to prompt my memory. I can remember the exact hue of her hazel eyes when kissed by the sun, her long wavy hair that holds as many colors as the pebbles along the riverbank where we sometimes walked together, her wide, full mouth that meant happiness and possibilities to me when she smiled, and utter desolation when she frowned.

The black and white newsprint picture is slightly blurred. Luckily her lips aren't where her forehead should be, or her eyes smudged so they look like she's been beaten, or any of the other grotesque print run errors we sometimes see in *The Riveredge Daily*. Gwen's face is only soft-focused and a bit faded, like a favorite book that's been read too many times, or a trusted pair of jeans that have grown threadbare in the knees.

The article says that Gwen's husband was photographed kissing a man outside a nightclub in the early morning hours. That's certainly surprising, but there's nothing in here warranting Shirley's remark. It's mostly background on the hometown girl we're all proud to call our own, and her catalog and *So Perfect* franchise. I turn to my computer to see if I can find out what Shirley meant.

GWENDOLYN GOLDEN SEEKS REFUGE IN RIVEREDGE headlines the online version of the paper, updated ten minutes ago. It says Gwen was never married to her partner. That doesn't seem criminal, and she always had a bit of a hippy streak. It also says Gwen is coming home. I can't help but wonder where she is at this very moment—if she's getting closer.

Last summer I watched a segment of Gwen working in her attic studio in that old North Carolina mansion. It must have been a hot day because she stripped off her smock and pulled her hair into an impromptu ponytail halfway through the segment. Her face was open and smiling when she answered a question, then lined in concentration when she turned back to her work. It was wonderful to watch her paint again, even if it was just on television. I admit that I not only watched the segment, I taped it too. But whether I've watched it back one time or a thousand is really no one's business.

The most prized possession I own is a sketch Gwen made of the two of us together, beside a gnarled old oak tree in Riveredge Park. She gave it to me before she went away to school a decade ago. Though I've only seen Gwen in person once during the intervening years, I admire that picture every single day.

"I'm bringing the car around to the side door to save you some steps." Taylor pokes his boyish blonde head into my office only long enough to say this. I want to yell out a protest, but what am I going to say? Steps are steps and we all know it.

"Can I help you?" Jessie asks from the doorway. I wonder where she gets her old-fashioned tweed suits that are as dusty as her hair color. I don't know why she annoys me so much, but she does.

"No thanks." I start to get up but she comes toward me anyway, like Shirley did, as if she knows better and is determined to help me whether I want help or not.

"Remind me Jessie, do you have to hold my dick when I take a piss?"

This is the only surefire line I have ever found to get the mosquito off me. As such, I have used it several times. I'm not proud of that fact; I would prefer that *No thanks* worked just as well. The unfortunate truth is that anything less than the dick line results in Jessie descending on me like a bad rash.

We close the deal that was months in the making. The first thing Taylor and I do when we get back is lock ourselves in my office and figure out appropriate bonuses for everyone. Taylor cautions me to be conservative. He always does. He's no hypocrite, though; he complains that he's getting too much, not just that everyone else is.

"Are you going to buy an engagement ring with your bonus money?" I ask.

Taylor's grin reminds me so much of the old me that it nearly brings tears to my eyes. He is optimism personified. He looks like he has his whole life ahead of him.

"That's exactly what I'm going to do!"

I reach over and pat his shoulder. "Congratulations! It's about damn time. Now what are you waiting for?"

"How about we go have a drink first to celebrate?" he asks, but I know he'd rather rush off to Carmen. Who wouldn't?

"Maybe I've got plans." I meant it as a joke but he smiles sadly before I catch him at it and shame him with a look that says, *I'm not only your big brother but your boss. Feeling sorry for me is not something I'm going to put up with.*

"Alright then, I'll see you at Siler's tomorrow night." Taylor is halfway out the door when he turns back. "Did you get a chance to look at that paper, by the way?"

"Go!" I tell him, pointing to the door.

I pick up the newspaper again and study the photo. It has been four years since I actually stood next to Gwen it person. In some ways it feels like yesterday, and in other ways it seems like it must have been another lifetime.

Gwen had been out of touch since she left for college. She had called when she came home a few times during freshman year, but I'd been working long hours, and between her schedule and mine we hadn't connected. I wrote her a letter sophomore year, but her address at school had changed and it was returned. I didn't really exist to her family, and Gwen and I never had mutual friends, so I couldn't think of anyone to ask for her contact information. I figured she'd call again while visiting, but she never did.

Six years since I had last seen her, she called out of the blue one day and asked if she could buy me lunch. Circumstances being what they were, I probably should have said no. But I said yes and we planned to meet in Riveredge Park. I saw her sitting on a bench when I pulled in. She had all the potential promise— or heartbreak—of a mirage.

I parked in the lot nearest her, but she hadn't noticed me yet. Her wavy hair spilled over the weathered slats of the wooden bench, and she sat with one long leg carelessly curled under her while she sketched intently.

I expected Gwen to vanish with every step I took, like she'd done in too many dreams. But she was there; she was real. A little closer and I could see the sketchpad in her lap, where she was drawing a magnificent oak tree near the river. Even though I recognized her style and knew it was her, I still half expected a different woman to look up when I said her name. It was Gwen, though, the same as ever. I almost fell over when she smiled at me.

Prior to that day, the last time I had spoken to Gwen was one of the worst days of my life, when I'd had to tell her that instead of going to the same college in North Carolina as her I was staying in Riveredge. The truth was that even with a full scholarship, I couldn't afford to go away after my dad collapsed at work earlier that summer. By the time he died, our family was in significant debt. The Riveredge Academy counselor helped me secure a local scholarship that meant I could attend college while I worked to help support my mom and brothers. I didn't explain the reasons to Gwen then. I didn't really get the chance.

"Hi stranger," she had said in Riveredge Park when she looked up from her bench. She dropped her sketchbook to the side and stood on her sleeping leg. It was an old habit of hers I had almost forgotten, sitting in a jumble and getting so immersed in her work she'd forget to change positions. She laughed as she held her arms out to me. I stood still for a moment, trying to fix the image in my mind.

"How are you?" she asked, looking at me with her penetrating hazel gaze, her arm still casually draped around my shoulder as she stamped her foot on the ground.

I can't remember how the conversation so quickly led to the fact that I was engaged, but sadly, it did. I remember Gwen taking her hand away and me wanting her to put it back.

I don't think Gwen ever realized how much I loved her. Maybe I didn't really fathom it either, not totally, until I saw her again. It made me realize that I couldn't marry Nancy. Though I loved her, I didn't feel about Nancy the way I felt about Gwen. I couldn't just pretend I did once I knew the difference.

Gwen said she had an announcement, too, and told me about the job she'd just landed painting designs for a new company called *So Perfect*. She looked up at me with her expressive eyes as our conversation waned.

"What's wrong?" I asked.

"I can't do lunch after all."

We walked along the river path for old times' sake. I hugged her goodbye near my car. I was still young enough to want to show her I'd made it, that I'd put myself through school and had worked so hard that I already owned my own company, and was doing well enough to have a nice sports car to boot. It certainly feels like more than four years ago when I remember those emotions, which seem so innocently juvenile to me now.

I wanted to kiss Gwen when she said goodbye. I wanted to tell her that I had always loved her. But first I had to break things off with Nancy, and by the time that was settled, Gwen's catalog had launched and I learned she was married.

"Irene called to reschedule your appointment. She said she didn't want to wait a whole week in between sessions, so you need to call her to find a time," Jessie says, coming into my office without knocking first, saying her piece before I was ready to listen.

I look at her very reluctantly.

"She said you can't avoid her that easily," Jessie reads infuriatingly slowly from the message she wrote on a sticky note. She hands it to me.

I wait for her to turn and leave. Finally she does.

I look at the note, which includes Irene's office and cell phone numbers. I picture Irene's pretty, cheerful face. Even when she's torturing me, she smiles. She has asked me out several times over the past few years, since we've been spending part of our Friday mornings together. Of course she feels sorry for me and asks out of pity. I think we both know, we all know, that my dating days are over.

I sigh as I pick up the newspaper again.

chapter four

gwendolyn

"No comment," I repeat from behind my dark sunglasses. I've said it over and over, from North Carolina to Michigan. Some of the questions thrown my way were hurled by housewives who glared at me like I was Hester Prynne, a few by business travelers who seemed insultingly amused. The only person I wanted to answer didn't even voice a coherent question; a little girl simply stared open-mouthed and pointed at me. I wanted to say, *I know! I'm as surprised and disappointed as you are by this whole mess. I really am.*

A few people smiled encouragingly and said words that were meant to bolster me. One woman said, "I know they're just telling lies about you." A man said, "Keep your chin up! The truth will out." I only thanked them nervously, not mentioning the fact that the truth already did out.

"No comment," I say again, but Megan steps on my foot with her full weight.

"If you say that to me one more time little sister, I guarantee you will regret it."

I pull my foot away and decide not to kick her with it. I need to stay on her good side. Now that our mother is gone, Megan is Dad's gatekeeper. If I want to see him, I have to get past her first. That's much easier said than done because my sister hates me. Megan is everything I'm not. She's petite and compact in a coiled kind of way, like she's ready to pounce, while I'm tall and lanky and more likely to saunter than make any sudden movements. She's an unmitigated entrepreneurial success, heading her own software company. She's a good daughter.

"Is there anything else you want to tell me so I don't have to read it in the paper?"

I hang my head and remove my sunglasses. I'm anxious to see my dad and try to pay the damn toll quickly. "I think you already know the gist. I don't write the blogs, or make up the recipes, or do the decorating. All I do is paint, and some of my paintings are used for the things we sell—like napkins, and cups, and linens."

"So you're no more or less of a fraud than they're saying?"

"You *knew* I was a fraud. Don't act so shocked!" I stop when Megan points sternly to Dad's closed door, like I stabbed him by raising my voice from ten feet away.

"You knew I wasn't married. You knew most of it wasn't true," I whisper.

Megan shakes her head without looking at me. This is far worse than yelling. She has her Mother face on. She's *disappointed.*

"It's a slippery slope, and I should have pulled you back when you ran for the edge. I blame myself."

I want to tell my sister that she's the only person who could take my dumb decisions and make them solely about her. I think of my dad on the other side of the door.

"Listen Meg, you couldn't have stopped me if you'd tried."

I see that she's softening a bit, which is almost as imperceptible to the naked eye as a vine growing up a stone wall.

"I'm sorry I'm an embarrassment. I really am." *I really am.* "Can I please go in and see him now?"

Megan huffs and puffs but she finally steps aside. I open the door to our dad's hospital room.

"So you'll stay here then, Gwennie?" I have been occupying a chair in the corner of my dad's room for half an hour. Nurses have been coming and going, prodding him, asking him questions, and writing things down. This is the first moment we've been alone. I pull my chair over to his bed and take his hand. I don't know why he assumes I'll stay.

"Stay here, lay low, and let the goddamn vultures forget about you, Do-Do," he says, giving my hand a squeeze.

If anyone else in the world called me Gwennie or Do-Do, I'd implore them earnestly to stop. My dad can call me anything he wants, though. He has always taken full advantage of my infinitely-shortenable name, using every variation possible. If he stopped, I would miss it.

He is alarmingly pale. Though I've always thought of my dad as a large man, he looks small lying down, with wires snaking off from him. He had a massive heart attack when he was only fifty-five and I was still in high school. We were all terrified to lose him, but he came through, lost weight, and became healthier than he had ever been before. He seemed so strong afterward; I think I froze him at his best in my mind. I hadn't really noticed that he was getting older. Then again, I haven't been around to notice.

When my mother died, I promised my dad that I'd come home more often. I didn't mean to break the promise. Her death had been a shock to us all. She was undergoing surgery for stomach cancer, but it was supposed to be routine. She was supposed to make it and keep fighting. It's so sad and hopeless to think of my dad there all alone, waiting to hear she had woken up and was ready to see him, but learning instead that she was suddenly gone forever.

I should have visited him more. I press his hand tighter and hold on.

Robin, the nurse, bustles in again. "He needs a nap," she says, shooing me away.

"Will you come back soon, GG?" he asks.

"Of course." I kiss his cheek.

Nurse Robin follows me into the hall. I can tell she's exasperated. Some patients and visitors have tracked me down in the cardiac unit and I've had to hide in my dad's bathroom. She leads the way to a small office and says I can use it as a waiting room, like I'll contaminate the general one.

I want to tell Nurse Robin that I'm sorry I'm making a nuisance of myself by simply existing here, where she's trying to get her work done. She doesn't give me a chance though. "Thanks," I say as she shuts the door.

I take advantage of the quiet to turn on my cell phone and file through new messages. I see that my boss, Trey Hammond has called five times. I breathe a sigh of relief that he's on top of all this. I should have known that Trey would already be working to control the damage to *So Perfect*. He will catch the falling franchise before it shatters. He'll explain the situation to the press so that everyone knows Armand and I really aren't so bad after all.

"Ms. Golden?" is how he answers my call. I haven't heard Trey call me that in four years, not since he'd happened to be in town on the day my photograph ran in the arts section of the *News and Observer* alongside a mediocre review of my exhibit of large-scale florals at a friend's gallery. Trey had worn an impressive suit and a charming smile, and he had said *Ms. Golden* much more beseechingly then.

"Yes, it's Gwendolyn," I reply.

"Please wait for a moment, Ms. Golden," he says in a tone so formal I almost giggle nervously. Or burst into tears.

When I met Trey at that gallery, I knew I'd be lucky to sell two paintings during the course of the entire exhibit. It wasn't like I had more gallery-owner friends to help me out, either. I hadn't taken my mother's practical advice and studied something useful in college, so I didn't have other options to fall back on. I had always dreamed of doing what I loved, and I naively thought my dedication and hard work would be enough to make it as a painter. By the time I met Trey I was beginning to accept that I'd have to get a day job soon. I wasn't proud of the fact that at age twenty-five my dad still bankrolled much of my life.

Is it shallow to admit that I'm a complete sucker for flattery? Not most kinds of adulation, because I downright distrust compliments about my looks—I still see myself as the gangly underweight teen Megan used to call Spaghetti Tree, but I'm a pushover if that same person admires my art. I get melty.

Trey cajoled me into going out to dinner soon after we met. I'm embarrassed to say how long it had been since anyone had wined and dined me, and it had been longer since someone had said I was a truly talented painter.

I take the phone away from my ear and check the display to make sure the call is still live. Trey must have me on mute. I wonder if I should hang up and call back in case there's a connection problem. I don't want to believe he just forgot about me altogether.

When I met Trey I was struggling to find my place as an artist in the world, and that is no easy feat. Imagine those endless *American Idol* line-ups outside of every audition venue, and think of all the hopefuls that couldn't come or didn't come that day, or who are outside of the age range. Extrapolate the notion for musicians, poets, writers, actors, anyone who wants to "make it" in a creative market with a next to impossible shot. Probably only crazy or naive people try. Even if one does buck the odds and achieves her dream, she learns along the way that there was at least as much luck and serendipity involved in her success as talent, probably far more. And getting there is simply the first step, because part of why she's put up on a pedestal in the first place is so that she can fall down again. Possibly the last few hours have jaded me, but I think there's some truth there.

"Ms. Golden?" Trey says, finally back on the line. "I'm sorry to have to tell you this, but I'm suspending your contract."

He pauses but I don't say anything. I feel my face burning red while I wait for more.

"Your pay is suspended indefinitely. Your company shares are frozen pending legal review. If you're needed for anything else on this end, we'll let you know."

He pauses again. Again I stay silent.

"The locks on the Scenic house will be changed. We'll have your personal items boxed up and shipped to you when you provide a forwarding address…"

He's not finished, but I am. I hang up.

Part of me can't believe this is happening. Another part has expected it every day for the past four years. While Trey insisted that the *So Perfect* life was a fun game that didn't have any losers, it was still creepy when people asked for my autograph for things I didn't really do, or thanked me for advice that really hadn't been mine to give.

I started down the *So Perfect* path believing what I wanted to believe. That's really the bottom line and I'm not making excuses. If I could go back and do things differently, of course I would. The trouble is, there's no going back.

Megan is suddenly standing in the doorway, frowning down at me like I'm a pile of vomit on her dinner plate. "Dad wants you to stay," she says.

I don't reply, since I'm sobbing my guts out.

"What's your plan? Are you going back there?" she demands.

I try to get control of my voice but it's touch and go. "They kicked me out. They're changing the locks."

Megan shuts the door and leans against it. "Listen," she says sternly, channeling our mother. "Dad isn't well. He wants you here. You can't stay with me and my family, obviously, and Dad's retirement community doesn't allow anyone under fifty-five to stay there. So you've got to get a place of your own."

I stare at her with my mouth open because my nose is too stuffed to breathe through. I want to ask why it's obvious that I can't stay with her. She has a big house in our old neighborhood. Is she afraid I'll infect her kids, like I'm a virus?

"How much money do you have?" she asks.

I don't want to admit that I'm not really sure. The expenses at the *So Perfect* house were covered. For the past four years I haven't paid a light bill or made a car payment. My wardrobe and salon services went on a company credit card, for which I never saw a bill. I think my *So Perfect* shares were worth a lot but Trey said they might not be mine any more. I haven't checked my accounts in a long time.

I shrug. Megan looks at me with total disgust.

"When did you become our mother?" I ask.

Megan sits down in the chair beside mine. She is silent for a long time before she says, "It would make Dad happy if you stayed in town for a while."

I study her to see if she's trying to manipulate me into staying. No. I can tell she wants me out of Riveredge, probably before I sully the entire water supply. I sniff.

"Personally, I'm already sick of your face," she says.

I nod, glad that she's at least telling the truth. "Back at ya."

"I'm too maxed to manage Dad's health issues along with everything else I've got going on. If you stay, you can help him."

The almost civil tone puts me off a bit. I'm used to Megan being a vicious bitch to me. "So having me here would help you?" I ask. I can't resist.

"I certainly don't want you here forever! But maybe it makes sense for a while. You're a pariah anyway, they won't take you back, and Dad needs some babysitting."

The idea actually doesn't sound horrible. "I suppose I could rent a place, if I could find something private…"

"Finding a private enough apartment might be an issue. But prices are so low here and everything's for sale, maybe you can buy something cheap to hole up in until this blows over, then sell for a profit once the market bounces back."

Megan has a talent for reducing everything to profit and loss. I sniff again.

"People know you here, Gwen. It might be easier for you here than somewhere else," she says, though it clearly hurts her to say it.

I realize that she's right. I'm not simply a fallen celebrity in Riveredge; I'm a real person, homegrown, one of theirs. I could be close to my dad. I could figure things out.

"How can I find a place?" I ask.

"I've dealt with Smith Walker on some commercial real estate deals. I bet he'd help you."

My face flushes at the mention of his name.

Megan takes a small laptop out of her tidy purse and turns it on. "Let's log on to your bank account and see how much you can spend."

Twenty minutes later, Megan jots down Smith's number on a piece of paper before turning off her computer. "See if he can meet you now. If he can, I'll drop you off."

"Meet me on a Friday night? I doubt it."

"I don't. I think he works all the time. If not, think of somewhere else I can drop you. The Holiday Inn was just renovated… I'm going to tell Dad we're leaving, but that you'll be back first thing tomorrow," she says on her way out the door.

"I want to say good night to him, too."

"You'll have all day tomorrow to say whatever you want. I'm in a hurry, so if you expect a ride somewhere, you better make a plan."

"This is Smith Walker." His voice brings back a thousand memories. I should have called a hotel when Megan left the room, but his name on the sheet of paper was irresistible.

"It's Gwen Golden. I'm sorry to bother you."

There's a pause, but it's mercifully short. "No bother at all. What can I do for you?"

"My sister Megan said you might be able to help me find a house here in Riveredge. I need one right away."

"I'd love to help you. Want to come by my office now and we'll talk about what you're looking for?"

"Now?"

"If you like."

He sounds like a safe haven somehow, like a dry cave on a stormy island my boat just crashed on, a warm fire I can curl up in front of on this cold Michigan night. I remember when I saw him four years ago, though, he was engaged. He's someone else's safe haven. "I'd be bothering you. It's a Friday evening…"

"Do you have a rental car to get over here?"

"Megan can drop me off. If you're sure it's okay."

"I'm sure it's okay. Will I see you soon?"

"Yes. Thanks so much, Smith."

"My pleasure," he says.

He was always such a gentleman.

*　　*　　*

"Stop apologizing!" I tell Armand on the phone. He called as soon as I hung up with Smith.

"I'm so sorry, kid!" he says again.

"I'm kind of relieved the jig is up, honestly. Where are you now? Have you spoken to your mom?"

He laughs weakly. "Well, I'm sitting in a rental car outside her building now. I've been in my fedora and ugly glasses disguise since I left the hotel and no one has recognized me. I'm in a cold sweat! I just know she's got the minister and her prayer circle waiting in there to drive the demons out of me."

I cringe because I fear he may be right.

"Did you speak with Trey?" I ask.

I hear Armand take a deep breath and let it out.

"What?" I ask.

"He said I have to do a television interview," Armand says.

"He didn't mention it to me."

"He only wants me to do it. He said the initial feedback is that I'm sympathetic. He wants me to tell what it was like being the brains behind your success."

"Are you going to?" I ask, my voice wavering a bit.

"Not if I can help it!"

He doesn't sound as tough as I'd like. I have never seen Armand stand up to Trey and actually win. On design decisions, sure, but not on anything that really mattered to Trey.

"Can he make you do it? He made us do some pretty cheesy things. Remember that freezing photo shoot at the beach?" We were rolling out a new line of picnic baskets, acrylic glasses, melamine plates, and linens. Armand had to get up at four a.m. to get the food prepared. It was a windy 60 degrees that day and wardrobe had us in bathing suits on Scenic Beach.

I wait for an answer but Armand doesn't have one right away. "I hope he can't make me do it," he finally says.

I wish Armand good luck with his mom and say a rushed goodbye when Megan opens the door to my tiny office hideaway.

She grabs my arm and pulls me roughly. "Come *on*! I brought my car around to a service spot and they're letting us out a back door to avoid the reporters."

"Reporters are here?" I ask.

She glares at me. "Yes. Apparently they're excited to cover something other than farm yields or high school basketball. Where am I dropping you?"

"Smith Walker's office first."

"There's no 'first.' I have to get home!"

"But then where will I go?" I hear the age-old whine I always get around Megan.

"Hell?" she suggests as she drags me toward the elevator.

"It's so nice to be back in the bosom of my loving family," I say, angry at my voice for breaking a little. The elevator doors take forever to open. Finally we step in.

Megan's grip on my arm tells me that she's mustering her last bit of patience and I had better not test her any further. When she speaks it's very measured and monotone, but I know if I pull her hair a tug or pinch her just the tiniest little bit she'd freak right out like when we were in high school.

"Listen, I've got a lot on my plate right now. I haven't seen my kids since I left for work yesterday morning. I didn't get home from the office until they were asleep last night, and when Dad called in distress this morning they hadn't woken up yet. My husband is unhappy with my schedule, to say the least, and I frankly have too much going on to make your problems my problems today, Gwen. You're a grown up, right? Can't you book your own hotel and call your own taxi after meeting with Smith?"

I pinch her lightly, only as a joke really. She doesn't take it very well.

"Sleep in the gutter for all I care! I honestly don't give a shit where you go or how you get there! And *you're* on Dad duty from now on because I'm so damn *sick* of this place I could *burn it down!*" Megan stops shouting when the elevator door opens to reveal a hospital staffer waiting to escort us to her car.

chapter five

smith

Jessie stares at me from my office doorway. She has been making bizarre faces, like a kid about to wet her pants, until I finally have no choice but to acknowledge her presence. I do so very reluctantly.

"Oh for God's sake. What?"

"The phone!" She shifts her weight from one foot to the other.

I can't imagine what has gotten Jessie so worked up. The only call that ever comes in after hours on a Friday is whichever of my brothers happens to be hosting dinner Saturday night. My family seems determined to watch over me, as if I'm not capable of taking care of myself anymore. They'd feed me every meal if I allowed it, but I've whittled them down to Saturday dinners and special occasions.

"Is it Siler?" I ask.

Jessie jumps up and down a little and points to the newspaper on my desk. "No! *She's* on the phone for you!"

I look at the picture in the paper and don't allow my hopes to rise, though they're stubbornly trying. Skeptically I ask, "Who?"

"Gwendolyn *Golden*! Should I put her through?"

I used to be so good at playing it cool. Of all the attributes I was born with and those I conjured practically out of thin air and honed, my ability to appear calm on the outside when my feelings coursed wildly on the inside has served me best. Unfortunately my emotions tend to run much closer to the surface now. I look down at Gwen's blurry photograph and back up to Jessie, who seems like she might very well burst with excitement.

"Well, I guess I'll take the call."

I wait for Jessie to disappear before I pick up the phone and attempt to muster my coolest cowboy tones. "This is Smith Walker."

"It's Gwen Golden." She says her name like she's confessing something terrible. "I'm sorry to bother you."

"No bother at all." Possibly the biggest understatement of my life. "What can I do for you?"

"My sister Megan said you might be able to help me find a house here in Riveredge. I need one right away."

OK, breathe. "I'd love to help you. Want to come by my office now and we'll talk about what you're looking for?"

"Now?" she asks.

Shoot, I overshot. "If you like."

"I'd be bothering you. It's a Friday evening…"

She sounds like she wants to come. She sounds tired. She sounds like she's having the worst day of her life. "Do you have a rental car to get over here?"

"Megan can drop me off. If you're sure it's okay."

If I'm sure it's okay? "I'm sure it's okay. Will I see you soon?"

"Yes. Thanks so much, Smith."

She sounds so grateful, so sweet, and so genuine. "My pleasure," I say. The second she hangs up, the conversation already seems unreal.

Jessie is flushed, and her eyes are so bright with excitement that she almost looks pretty when she pokes her head into my office again. She must've been perched over the indicators on the phone to fly in here the instant mine went dark. Jessie's face tells me that if that call was a figment of my imagination, then I'm sharing her dingbat fantasy. In order to infuriate her, I try to look as if I'm bored, as if this is a very, very boring day.

"What's the matter, Jessie?" I ask. Boredly.

"What did she *say*? How do you know her? Oh my goodness! Is she coming here?"

"I didn't know you were such a fan of Gwen's."

"Well, I don't know that I'm a *fan*, really. But she's so

famous! And today she's more famous than ever! This is the most exciting thing that's happened in Riveredge in ages. And she called *you*, Smith Walker!"

If the mere idea of a famous person calling has gotten Jessie this loopy, I certainly can't risk her seeing Gwen in person.

"Listen," I say, trying to make an impression on Jessie, which is about as easy as making an impression on a slab of cured concrete. "I don't want you mentioning that phone call to anyone. She's not coming here," I lie. Unfortunately I am a really bad liar.

"Not ever?" she asks with her eyes narrowed.

"Probably not. Why would she?"

"She called you."

Jessie suspects I'm lying, I can tell.

"Well, if she ever did visit here when you're working, I'd want you to treat her like anyone else coming through the door. Okay?"

"I could ask for her autograph, right? And have my camera handy, just in case?" Jessie's forehead is wrinkled in concentration.

"No, Jessie!"

"Are you sure she's not coming now?"

"No," I lie again. I only lie when it seems kinder than the truth. I want to spare Jessie the pain of knowing she'll miss seeing a real life celebrity, though she's already proven she'd act insane if given the chance.

"Okay, she's coming," I admit, because Jessie's got her arms crossed in that infuriating way she sometimes does, like she might just stand there and block my way all evening if I don't fess up to what's really going on. "But you have to leave," I add.

Her sudden smile falls into a comically exaggerated frown.

"What are you doing here so late anyway?" I ask.

"I was finishing the paperwork for the deal you closed today! And *this* is the thanks I get? Do you know what it's like day in and day out working for you, Smith Walker, you arrogant ass?"

I don't know that I have ever heard Jessie swear before. I'm impressed. "Unpleasant?" I suggest.

She chortles and I'm afraid she might cry. I watch a crazy set of emotions race each other over her mousy face before she settles on barely-controlled, hurt-feelinged hysterics. "The *one time* there seems to be a perk and you're making me go home!"

"Bye now, honey," I say. "And make sure everyone else has gone home before you let the door close behind you."

For a mouse, Jessie makes as much noise as twenty elephants as she packs up and gets ready to leave. I hear her yell at a straggler by the big conference room and drop a coffee mug in the kitchen before she stomps up to my door again.

"Yes, dear?" I ask. I find it annoys Jessie to use terms of endearment when she's angry. It's the only time I use them.

"At least get an autograph for me!" she demands. "And one for my mom."

I sigh heavily. I was hoping she'd swear at me again.

Just when I thought I was alone in our offices, Taylor appears in my doorway.

"I saw your light on." He holds out a fancy little box and opens it to show me a diamond ring.

"Carmen will love it," I say.

He beams. "Let's go have a drink to celebrate."

"Sorry, but I just got off the phone with a beautiful woman who says she's on her way over to see me," I say.

Taylor frowns.

"Really! Gwen Golden needs some real estate help," I tell him, because the line of joking just wasn't working out. He was looking sad, and I was starting to feel it.

"You're kidding!" he says, seeming nearly as star struck as Jessie.

Since she's been a celebrity, I guess I have also thought of Gwen as *the* Gwendolyn Golden, the *So Perfect* one. I have regularly seen her on television, just like everyone else in Riveredge has. On the phone, though, Gwen sounded like herself—not a personality, but a person I've known most of my life.

"She looks like a supermodel," Taylor says.

"Well she was always as tough as she was pretty," I say. "On my first day at Riveredge Academy, she actually stood up to a bully and kept me from getting expelled."

"Is that right?" he asks, pulling up a chair like I'm going to tell him a nice long story. I'm ready to shoo him out when his phone rings. "Sorry, I've got to take this," he says, stepping into the hall.

But now that I brought it up, I can't seem to get that first day of school out of my mind.

I was nervous at the newness of everything, from the students, to the teachers, to the buildings. I had been admitted to prestigious Riveredge Academy on an academic scholarship to begin sixth grade. An ethic of the school was to court the very best students in the region, whether or not they had the means to pay. The year I started, I was the only newcomer attending on a full scholarship. My parents had nothing but love and five sons, of which I was the oldest.

Most of my fellow sixth graders had attended Riveredge Academy from preschool on. Scholarship kids were admitted only in sixth or ninth grade, so I was easy to spot.

There was a lot of talk about confidentiality from the admissions director at my personalized orientation. She said everyone would do their best to make me feel at home. But adults see the world differently than adolescents. Before our homeroom teacher came in that first day, one of the country club, academy-since-preschool kids cornered me.

His name was Elton Jorgensen, and to this day I attribute my extreme distrust of men with dimples to him. He smiled with only his mouth, his eyes were as cold as I'd ever seen on a kid. He said, "I'm Elton Jorgensen. And you'll be known around here as Scholarship."

"Smith Walker," I said in a calm voice, holding out my hand for him to shake. Inside, I was already boiling. I willed my hand to be steady, though, and it was.

Jorgensen's voice was calm, too. Calm and mean. "You'll answer to 'Scholarship.'"

"Smith Walker is my name." I put my hand on my hip and

turned to face the rest of the class who had gathered around as if we were a television set. I looked in every pair of eyes that were willing to meet mine, which amounted to most of the kids, except those who stood close to Elton and seemed to be waiting for him to tell them how to act.

I was used to a tough set of characters in my part of town, and I was tall for my age. I thought Elton Jorgensen with his turned up collar and dimples was probably just a smug jerk. I still didn't like how cold his eyes were.

Jorgensen fell to the floor just as the teacher entered the room. He said I'd hit him, and my stomach sank. He was quite a convincing actor and this was almost literally his turf; I had noticed on my orientation tour that morning a new football field and six-lane running track called Jorgensen Field. The boys who had appeared to be awaiting orders a moment before immediately backed up Elton.

"He hit him."

"We all saw it."

Before I had left that morning, my parents said I needed to be on my very best behavior. I could tell they were nervous for me. I knew part of it had to do with money and opportunity, and being proud of me, and hoping I liked it there for my own good and for my future. My dad worked a factory job, often taking double shifts for the overtime pay. I knew my parents wanted me to have more options than they'd had.

I saw that my mom was apprehensive for me, but she was proud, too, that I was selected to attend Riveredge Academy despite the fact that we were poor. Looking at Elton Jorgensen, I feared that my parents' pride would be short lived and I'd be sent home within the hour, making room for someone who'd remember his place.

Then I saw Gwen Golden for the first time. She was almost as tall as I was, I remember, and her hair was very blonde and quite short. She had a look of quiet determination on her face that was formidable. For a moment I thought she was going to stick up for Elton, too, thus ensuring my expulsion.

As she strode over, I backed up to get out of her way but

was stopped by a desk. She crossed her arms over her chest and frowned. I was scared the frown was meant for me.

"Elton insulted this boy, Mr. Morton! He threw himself on the floor to get Smith Walker in trouble. I saw the whole thing," Gwen told the teacher in a fiery voice.

While a few others found their tongues and seconded Gwen's version of events, and Elton and his friends tried to stick to their story which was rapidly falling apart, Gwen turned to me.

"It's good to meet you, Smith Walker," she said with a warm smile, offering her hand to help me up.

"You need to get out of here," I tell Taylor when he steps back into my office.

"I'll stay and let your old friend in first," he says like it's necessary, like I need him to do something as simple as that.

"Bullshit!" I mean to end the conversation, not to hurt my baby brother's feelings. I make an effort to smile in a way that says *I'm sorry* without actually having to say it. "Go bring that ring to Carmen," I tell him.

I know that Gwen should be arriving soon, so I begin to make my way to the vestibule as soon as Taylor leaves. I suppose I must have warmed up my reminiscing muscles because more memories of Gwen vie for my attention with every step. And for whatever reason, the night of junior prom takes over my mind as I slowly walk down the hall.

The junior prom was traditionally a lavish affair at the school, with most kids arriving in limousines or their parents' best cars. The boys rented tuxedoes and bought their dates flowers and took them to the most expensive restaurants. I couldn't compete with any of that, but I was too young and too proud to try and explain it to Gwen. Instead, I simply didn't ask her to go with me. She didn't seem hurt but perhaps she was. We never discussed it, but as the prom neared we spent less time together. I think the feelings of teenagers are like icebergs—only about ten percent actually break the surface.

I'd heard Gwen had been asked to the prom by several guys but had turned them all down, and that she planned to go with a group of girls. I had been spending junior prom night at home, ostensibly studying, but really wondering if I should have just explained my situation to Gwen, or if she hated me now, or what it would be like to be rich and able to do what the other kids at school did.

Mrs. Closs, our next-door neighbor, was a waitress at the Riveredge Country Club. Sometimes she brought extra food home, and if it happened to be chicken, she brought it over to us. She had grown up on a chicken farm in West Virginia and had lost her taste for it. Our family always had plenty to eat, but with five boys, my mother didn't turn down free food from the Riveredge Country Club. It usually went straight from the container into our growing bodies without touching plates or a warming oven.

Mrs. Closs had been working the prom that night, but when she tried to leave the club her car wouldn't start. My dad was on third shift at the time, and my mom was already asleep, so I answered the phone when Mrs. Closs called. She asked if I would please come and get her.

Sometimes I remember growing up as one embarrassment after another—like a comedy of errors without any humor. I know that's not really the way it was, because I have wonderful memories of family times and there was a tremendous amount of laughter in our small house. I think spending my days with rich kids was just hard for me, being different and proud, and feeling so responsible to my brothers and parents. Every morning I went from from being a big deal at home, to being less than nobody at school, then back to important again by the end of the day.

I didn't want to pull through the enormous wrought iron gates of the Riveredge Country Club in my beat-up car that I was never sure would start, but I had promised to bring Mrs. Closs home. It was the right thing to do, the honorable thing, so why with all these years between that earnest, embarrassed boy and my grown-up self does my face still turn red and my pulse quicken when I think back to that night?

I stood in the doorway of the ballroom that looked like something from another world to me, so ornate and sparkling, like a scene from a magical book. I tried to adjust my eyes so that I could quickly find my neighbor and get out of there before I was discovered and maybe broke the spell.

I looked along the sidelines, expecting to see Mrs. Closs at one of the refreshment tables, serving from one of the enormous punch bowls. Elton Jorgensen pointed me out to his date, smirking, while I continued to look around for my neighbor. I saw Jorgensen's face fall and turned to look where he looked.

I caught my breath. Gwen was coming toward me, like a vision. Her hair was long by then, with more shades of gold woven through it than a sunrise. She wore a strapless silver gown and long white gloves. They were satin; I remember the way the cool fabric felt when she put her hand in mine.

"I can't believe it!" she said. She seemed amazed to see me. "It's the last dance, so come on," she said, tugging me toward the dance floor.

"I'm not going out there like this." I nodded my chin down to indicate my clothes, but didn't take my eyes from hers.

"You have to. I just saw a falling star out the window and I wished for you. When I looked up, there you were!"

It would be nice to say that I danced gracefully and forgot about my ripped jeans, old shirt, and dirty tennis shoes. That Gwen and I marched to the center of the floor while everyone parted to behold this couple who were so clearly meant for each other. But I've never been much of a dancer, certainly not now, but not then either, and I couldn't forget how out of place I was. I let Gwen lead me out to the floor, but only to the periphery, where I'm sure we were either invisible or derisively acknowledged by those who noticed us.

But for those few minutes, I closed my eyes and concentrated on how Gwen's satin dress felt under my hands, how her hair smelled like I imagined a tropical garden might on a moonlit evening, how her beauty made the other girls just look plain and silly, and most of all how those words had sounded when she said them to me: *I wished for you.*

I think those were the best moments I've ever had. Maybe it's sad for a grown man to admit that his adult life has been trumped by a few minutes when he was just a skinny kid of seventeen. I don't know. But when I thought my life was ending on that awful night more than three years ago, as I lay bleeding on the pavement, those were the very moments I tried to conjure. Not a round of happy birthday sung over a lit cake when I was four…or fishing with my Grandpa on the glinting-in-the-sun waters of Lake Huron when I was twelve…or watching my mother's face when I bought her the condo of her dreams a few years prior…but that one dance. When I thought I was having my last thoughts on this earth, I wanted to remember holding Gwen Golden's satiny waist with her white-gloved hand in mine, looking into her smiling eyes, and hearing her say, "I wished for you."

chapter six

armand

Looking out from my rental car onto the big paved lot, I swear I see kids jumping and laughing. My hung-over mind is playing tricks. It's January, which means winter even in Praiseville, South Carolina. It's too cold for jumping today. It's already dark, and it doesn't seem like a single soul is out and about.

I probably wouldn't recognize anyone even if it was a nice June evening and people were sitting outside. I've lost touch with my old neighborhood. The only thing that brings me back is when my mother calls and says I have to get over here. That doesn't happen too often.

I hear those kids that aren't really there again. Maybe the cold is freezing out my brain cells while I sit in this tiny car watching my breath, making me remember things I'd long since forgotten. Making me think of jump rope, of all the crazy things I could be thinking of on such a crazy day as this. Now that I dove in, I may as well swim a little.

Jump rope was all the rage on my street when I was a kid, and I loved it. Either I didn't notice that only the girls jumped, or I didn't mind being the only boy out there. No one teased me about jumping rope, or if they did I don't remember. It was like a party every day, singing, swinging the rope, jumping, and laughing as things got going faster and faster. I was pretty good, and I made up lots of new rhymes for us to sing.

I remember one summer day in particular, when I was about seven years old. Funny how memories will come back at odd times and just tap you on the shoulder and say, "Hey, look at me! I said *look* at *me*. Look at me right now whether you want to or not."

That day, my mom had sent me out to play while she stayed inside and prayed with the minister. After he'd gone away, she came and sat down on the step to watch us. She smiled and tapped her feet through a few songs. I'd been working out a new one, so I thought I'd go ahead and sing it for her as a solo act, because it wasn't every day that she came outside and sat her considerable self down to watch me play.

In retrospect I know it would've gone better as a chorus. And looking back, I realize I shouldn't have taken the songwriting credit right up front.

Like I said, memories are the craziest things sometimes. Though I can't remember anything at all about the French and Indian war, the name of a single President between Jackson and Lincoln, or one certain weekend during college that left me with a small tattoo I'm not going to mention again, I still remember every word to that rhyme I sang my mama when I was about seven years old.

It was a sunny day and she was smiling down at me and everything seemed happy and nice. Two of my girlfriends started swinging the big rope, and I jumped in and sang, real loud and proud. The song went like this:

> *I don't want to marry Mary*
> *I'd rather go steady with Stu*
> *Randy might come in handy*
> *Peter would know what to do*
> *No I don't want to marry Sherry*
> *Though I'd like to hang out with Hugh*

I honestly did not know that my mother could move so fast. I'm surprised she didn't dislocate my shoulder when she pulled me out of that jump rope and up the stairs, slamming the door once she got me inside. I didn't realize at first that the song had made her mad. I didn't know what in heaven's name was going on.

I got a lecture and a whooping that didn't explain much.

She reminded me that I had tried on her lipstick the year before, and had called Donnie Wahlberg from New Kids on the Block handsome, and more things I'd long since forgotten about. Seemed like she'd been holding on to stuff that had made her mad, and she gave it to me all at once.

She prayed over me something fierce, and the only thing I took away from it was that she was angry with me, and that somehow she thought I was dirty. Your mama thinking you're dirty makes a mighty large impression on you when you're seven years old. Let me just go ahead and say that, in case you didn't know.

A long while after the black and blue handprints on my bottom had faded away, I sang that song again. I had the good sense to keep it quiet and hidden, though, and to only sing it to myself. I also added a few lines:

> *Maybe someday I'll marry Larry*
> *But never if my mama knew*

I have to keep reminding my legs to walk up to her door. I think if it were up to them, they'd turn around and run the other way.

"Armand!" My mother says gruffly after I talk my finger into ringing the bell.

She looks both angry and scared of me—or of something, anyway. She peeks up and down the street before pulling me inside with one large and swift arm. She shuts the door and throws the locks.

"Ma'am," I say, attempting to hug her. She stands there like a mountain of solid rock and makes a formidable ledge by folding her arms. I give up and look down at the floor. The braided brown rug is a hateful old thing. I spent too much time studying it over the years while my mother glared at me. It's brow-beaten and shame-colored.

"Reporters were here today, Armand. They knocked on my door! I had to unplug the telephone because there were so many calls."

She sounds like she thinks I arranged it all myself just to

harass her. She stares at the counter and I do too, and indeed there's an unplugged telephone sitting there.

I have an overwhelming desire to giggle nervously. It's a terrible coping mechanism; it must be a form of fight or flight or something. I always had the same reaction in church when the topic was fire and brimstone. I paid for it afterward, and it was never worth it. I didn't want to laugh in the first place; I just couldn't help it.

I manage to cough the urge to giggle away this time.

"I'm really sorry about the reporters," I say as I look around. The place is so small. Of course, I've gotten used to eight thousand square feet of pure luxury, with soaring ceilings and huge windows in every room. But I don't remember this apartment ever feeling so much like a shoebox with the lid crammed on too tight.

My mother sits down in her chair. You can tell it's her chair at a glance, because it has been molded to her body over the years. I kid you not, it shows each ass cheek. I wouldn't make up such a thing about my own mama.

"Armand, they say you're *deviant*."

"Who says I'm *deviant*?"

"The new minister was by today. Old Reverend Sugarbaker died last year, remember?" She whispers the last part and I see the pain on her face. I know Reverend Sugarbaker meant a lot to her, though she never cared much for his wife.

I don't say anything. What in heaven's name am I supposed to say to *deviant*? I'm so mad I might let myself go ahead and giggle out loud if I felt like it. I don't, though.

She points to the sofa and I sit down.

"Tell me that news story is wrong now. I know you're married, I have this picture to prove it." She holds out the wedding photo I sent her. "Tell me the story is wrong, Armand."

I hear some old platitudes in my head, like "you made your bed, you better lie in it," and "you reap what you sow," and I know it's my own fault that my mother believed I was married. None of these thoughts are very helpful right now, though. "Should have thought of that before." Yes, I should have. I really should have.

I silently practice what I want to say. *I know you believe certain crazy, small-minded things that make being my mother hard on you.* No, that's not a good start. *I've been in the damn closet all this time because you locked me in there with fifty deadbolts like a dangerous lion in a cage, when you know I'm really just a pussycat.* No, still not good. I like the metaphor but it won't help. *I am thirty-one years old and it's high time I start living my own life. I lied to you before and I'm sorry. But I am done lying, ma'am, whether you like it or not.* Yes, that's the one.

"Armand? Tell me the story is wrong."

Lenny Nelson and I formed a study club in tenth grade. Funny thing was, no matter how much time we spent locked quietly away in his room or mine, our grades both stayed pretty poor. My mom started looking at Lenny funny after a while when she used to say how nice it was that we studied together, because I'd never had much interest in poring over books before I found Lenny. After the second round of report cards came home showing no improvement, she started being a little short with Lenny and didn't offer him sodas or snacks anymore.

One day when we got home from school and she wasn't there, Lenny said he was glad because he was starting to be afraid of her. I remember wondering what in heaven's name had taken him so long; I couldn't remember a single day in all my life when I hadn't been afraid of my mother. I said let's go in my room and study history a little while.

She must have come in real quiet because I didn't hear a thing. She picked my lock and swooped in so fast we didn't have time to open our books or put ourselves back together properly.

As big as she was, my mother could not spank a six-foot tall young man even if I was beanpole skinny back then. But that wasn't her only option, as I well knew. I got myself together and started to run and told Lenny he'd better do the same, but he wasn't as quick as me. By the time she'd grabbed the broom handle I was almost to the door. She still got several good licks in before I made it out of her reach.

Poor Lenny.

I remember being so scared to come home I almost didn't.

Right now I wish to God I hadn't.

"Armand? I told you to tell me the story is wrong. Now."

I look her in the eyes. She is my mother. If your mama doesn't love you no matter what, then who is gonna? Just tell me that.

"You know the truth already, ma'am. You've always known the truth."

She stares at me until I lower my eyes. This isn't about a mother's love to her. I think she believes it's about my soul. Or hers.

"Then I know the story is wrong," she says.

Maybe I'm a coward and maybe I'm a pragmatist and maybe I think that broom handle is likely still in its place in the closet. I don't know why, but I don't argue. What can I say that would make any difference to her?

I sit there a while and listen to her talk about Gladdy Prinster and the rest of her church lady friends, and about her swollen ankles, as if this were any old visit on any old day. When I think I've sat there long enough to do a thousand penances and pay my purgatory in advance, I tell her I've got to go.

She says that's a good idea. For once, we see eye to eye.

chapter seven

gwendolyn

Megan doesn't say a word as she drives us out of the hospital parking lot. I don't dare speak or turn on the radio for fear that my sister will slap me. I steal glances, though. She has frown wrinkles all around her mouth like our mother had. I thought the latter's had come from a lifetime of smoking, but I've never once seen Megan light up. One of the many things my sister seems to have inherited from our mother is a horrible propensity to look like she just swilled week-old cold coffee.

Megan is wearing a business suit, though she said she never made it into the office today. She rigidly grips the steering wheel at the ten and two position, staring through the windshield like a fighter pilot under enemy fire. Seeing her tension makes me stretch out my arms and legs in front of me before letting them flop where they may.

She takes her eyes from the road only long enough to glare at me.

The assumption that little girls want to emulate their big sisters is bullshit, at least in my case. I have always tried to do the exact opposite of whatever Megan does. She used to say that I had been dropped off in a basket at the front door as an infant and didn't really belong with the Golden family. I wanted to believe her because it would have explained so much. I was completely different from my mother and Megan. It would have been nice to imagine a long, lanky mother out there in the world, perhaps missing me. I couldn't truly believe it, though, because of my dad.

"Have you kept in touch with Smith Walker?" Megan suddenly asks.

"Why would I?" I hear the defensiveness in my voice. I always used to sound this way when the subject of Smith came up. I had to, because my family was always on the offensive.

Megan shrugs like she couldn't care less either way. I wonder why in the hell she bothered to ask then.

This is truly the weirdest day I have ever had. This morning Stuart Bolder denounced me from my front lawn in Scenic, North Carolina, and now I'm in Michigan, minutes from seeing Smith Walker, my consistent regret in life. I want to know what Smith is like now, if he's happy. I want to know if he has children, and if he does, if they resemble him. I want to know what his wife is like.

I was surprised when Megan said she has worked with Smith. In school she had acted like he was an inconvenient and unseemly nuisance, like a big wad of gum on the bottom of her shoe. I try to formulate a casual question to ask about him that doesn't show how much I really want to know, but Megan's cell phone rings.

She answers the call on speakerphone. "I'm on my way!" she says.

"OK," her husband Kyle replies. He sounds tired. "How's Gordy doing?"

"It looks like he'll be alright." Megan exhales like she's been holding her breath all day long.

"Good. I see your sister made it to town?"

"Yup," Megan says with a sigh.

"Do I have to get the guest room ready?" Kyle asks, sounding like a put-upon housemaid.

"No! Reporters gather around her like flies on garbage. We don't need that."

"Where's she staying?" Kyle asks.

"A hotel, I guess, until she finds a more permanent place… it's a long story. I'm dropping her off at a realtor to help her find an inexpensive house."

"She's with you now?" he asks.

"Hi, Kyle," I say.

"Oh, hi. Hey, if you're looking for houses, I heard of one in the Hidden Pines subdivision that's supposed to be nice. A librarian at the university has to sell it before the bank forecloses."

"Who?" Megan demands quickly.

"One of the university librarians," he replies, sounding as defensive as I felt when Megan asked about Smith. I suppose she brings that out in people.

"Do you know the street?" I ask.

"I think she said it was on Hidden Lakes Drive."

"OK, thanks," I tell him.

"How much longer before you get here?" Kyle asks.

"Fifteen minutes?" Megan replies.

"Dinner is ready now, but we'll wait."

Megan clicks the phone off and I stare at her. For a moment there while she talked to Kyle she looked almost soft, nearly kind. She glares at me, having switched back so fast I didn't see the transformation, only that she's got her nasty, rabid bitch face on again.

"What?" she demands.

"Nothing. You said you've worked with Smith before?"

"Yes."

"How is he to work with?" I ask, trying to draw out my words to offset her clipped, one syllable response.

"Unlike most of the realtors I've dealt with in this town, he's at least honest," she says.

I'm encouraged by that longish, semi-civil answer, but before I can ask another question Megan switches on the radio loudly, with the obvious intention of tuning me out.

I lean my head on the back rest and close my eyes. I try to remember the details of Smith's face. He was always handsome, but there are lots of handsome guys in the world. Smith had something beyond that, a special quality that set him apart. This probably sounds incredibly cheesy, but I think Smith Walker is innately good. Like good-good. Not saintly, thank goodness, but kind and helpful and truthful good. Even Megan, who is barely human, just said he was honest. When we were growing up, though, she agreed with my parents that he wasn't worth noticing.

"Do you still spend a lot of time at the club?" I ask Megan as we pass by the grand front entrance of the Riveredge Country Club. I shout the question but she still ignores it.

At the end of my senior year I tried to get my parents and Smith together. I'd gotten my mother's promise that she would be civil if I asked Smith to dinner at the club. I tried to impress Dad with the fact that Smith had been offered full academic scholarships to several schools, though I knew my father was more impressed by sports than academia. Since I was going to the same university as Smith, my parents agreed it would be wise to get to know him at least a little before we were gone.

I always wanted to get to know Smith's family, too. Over the years there was invariably an excuse why it wouldn't work out for me to visit his house. I had met his parents and brothers at awards ceremonies where Smith took top honors. On those occasions he'd presented me rather formally, and I thought it was incredibly sweet. His brothers were cute and his parents seemed very shy. That he never brought me home was another factor that made me wonder if our relationship meant more to me than to him.

The dinner at Riveredge Country Club was a special send off for graduating seniors and their families. The next morning I was leaving to backpack through Europe with a group of girlfriends, so this would be my last chance to see Smith for months. He was working that afternoon, but said he'd meet us at 6:00 at the club. I waited by the ornate doors until 6:30, but he never arrived.

I left the next morning without having received an apology from Smith. I flirted my way through Europe trying to forget him at first, but it didn't work. I spent the last few weeks moping and counting the hours until I would be back home. I called Smith right away when I arrived, dreaming of a wonderful reunion. Instead we had a tear-filled thirty-second conversation. He told me he wasn't going away to school after all. I didn't wait for him to explain his reasoning. I was hurt and heartbroken and

I hung up on him.

I had adored Smith all through middle and high school. His last minute change in college plans was a devastating blow. In an effort to move on, I dated men that ranged from a lot like Smith, to the exact opposite, but I never could get him out of my mind. I called him when I visited home freshman year, but he didn't want to see me.

Smith Walker has been my model of what a man should be. I'm not saying that has necessarily been a good thing for me. If the first bite of cake I ever tasted was from the best baker in the world who then closed up shop, I'd have to go through a hell of a lot of cakes to come across one half as good. Maybe I'd think it would've been better to have tasted mediocre cake first, so I'd have a more realistic comparison.

I did fall in love once after Smith. He was an associate art professor who flattered me where it counted: he said I was one of the most talented young painters he'd ever seen. Jeremy was a philosophical guy with a goatee to prove it. Mostly Jeremy and I stayed in bed when we were alone, but when we were in small groups with other students in a coffee shop or someone's rental house, he loved to discuss art. I thought he was so wise, cultured, and handsome. We went out for a year before I learned he was married.

"Riveredge Park," I say as we drive past it.

"What?" Megan barks.

"Riveredge Park!" I yell over her music. I point back at it.

She looks at me with such profound annoyance it almost has a righteously indignant quality to it, as if I made a racial slur, or tortured a kitten, instead of having simply interrupted her music for a moment to say something useless.

"Riveredge Park!" I yell again for Megan's benefit.

Riveredge Park is the last place I saw Smith. Though I hadn't seen him for six years by then, I came back to town to tell Smith about my new job. The catalog was soon to launch, and though I doubted he'd ever see a copy of *So Perfect*, I wanted him to know that Armand and I were only posing as a married couple for marketing purposes. That's when I learned he was engaged.

Another four years have passed and here I am, about to see him again.

Megan abruptly switches off the radio. "You're here," she says, pulling up to my favorite downtown Riveredge building. The bottom floor has letters that spell *Smith Walker Agency* in black, in a reserved font attached to the aged red brick above the lobby doors.

I'm so nervous. I suddenly wish that I looked better. I wish Armand were here to make me camera ready, or more importantly, ready for the eyes of Smith Walker.

chapter eight

smith

Gwen flips off her sister Megan, who peels out of the parking lot. Their deranged enmity used to truly terrify me. Megan still scares me when I see her barreling through town; she's so much like her mother. Gwen looks gorgeous as she walks to the door. I struggle to hold it open for her but she stops cold about five feet away.

"What happened?" she asks.

This is what I dreaded. I point inward past the lobby, into the quiet anonymity of my working world, but she stands still.

"An accident?" she asks, slowly coming toward me again without taking her eyes from mine, until she's touching the long scar along the left side of my face.

I nod yes.

I'm relieved she doesn't look down at my left leg. Despite my heroic attempts, no matter what my physical therapist Irene may call them, I have to drag it along everywhere I go now, like old hopes, like missed opportunities. Or, as my brother Jones more poetically puts it, "like a sack a bad potatoes."

"What happened?" Gwen asks. Her eyes seem even bigger than I remember. They're outlined in dark circles; she looks exhausted.

"Come on now. Let's get you inside before anyone finds out you're here."

She holds the door for me but I insist she go first.

"How's your dad?" I ask as I make my way up the hall. Gwen stays with me at my snail pace.

"It looks like he'll be OK," she says.

Gwen folds herself into a chair with both legs tucked under her when we reach my office. I make my way around the desk and begin the twenty-step process of trying to sit down while keeping my cane in reach and not letting the chair slip out from under me. Once I'm seated, she holds on to the desk and wheels closer to me. I can smell her hair: coconut, maybe lime, and antiseptic—that last is probably from Riveredge Memorial. I suppress a shudder.

"So will you tell me what happened? Or don't you like to talk about it?" she asks.

I hate talking about it. I hate everything about it.

"An SUV ran a red light while I was crossing the street late one night."

"And you never saw it coming?" she asks.

I want to tell her that's right, it all happened too fast for thought. But in truth it was the longest moment of my life. I saw the driver realize too late, and it felt like I had years to ponder the pain to come.

I look away from her face. "No. I saw it coming."

She shakes her head and closes her eyes. "I'm so glad you're okay."

I would chuckle derisively if anyone else had said that, but Gwen appears utterly sincere.

"Coffee?" I ask to change the subject.

"Do you have anything stronger? Like vodka, or a pistol?" she laughs and I'm relieved the conversation has shifted to her.

I hoist myself up to standing and head back out of the office. Eventually I return with two beers from the break room. "Here," I say, handing her a bottle after twisting off the cap. "If you want a glass I can make another trip. Be back in a jiffy."

She smiles. I make my way around my desk and do the twenty steps again.

Gwen takes a long swig and I remember she could drink as much as me when we were teenagers and had scored a bottle of wine to drink by the river.

"This is perfect. I don't know when I last had a beer,"

she says.

"All champagne lately, huh?" I push my chair under the desk to hide my leg. I know it makes people sad.

"Water mostly. Armand tries to stay away from alcohol, so I've practically been a teetotaler for the past four years."

I want to ask if the online article was right, if she and Armand only pretended to be married. But the world of *So Perfect* seems very far from here. It strikes me as both bizarre and somehow normal that I don't want to bring up the topic so many people have been talking about today, to the woman they have been discussing.

"So, you want to find a place in Riveredge?"

"Megan says it's my turn to look after our dad. She also said there are lots of houses on the market, and maybe I can get a good deal on one that I can sell for a profit later."

"It's definitely a buyer's market. What's your budget?"

"Megan and I logged on to my bank account at the hospital and talked it over. She said I can spend $200,000." Gwen grimaces, like she's mortified by that number. "I think the house in Scenic was worth $2,000,000," she adds.

I'm tempted to tell Gwen that $200,000 is a hell of a lot of money to a hell of a lot of people. That the house I grew up in with four brothers—where my brother Siler now lives with his family—still isn't worth half that in today's market, even after he's worked hard to make it as nice as it can be. But Gwen looks tired and repentant and frankly afraid. She lowers her head onto her folded arms resting on my desk.

"Armand wants to move here, too?" I ask, trying to sound casual.

"Why would he?" she asks, looking up.

I almost crack a smile at her predicament. I don't think Gwen is any more a natural liar than I am. I wonder how on earth she got herself into this mess. "Isn't he your husband?"

She makes a face like she just smashed her toe. "We pretended to be married. It was part of the marketing plan for *So Perfect*. I know it sounds very bad, but at the time it didn't seem…" She puts her head back down and soon I see her shoulders shake a bit. She sniffles and I slide the box of tissues on my desk close to her.

I could have kissed Gwen that day in Riveredge Park four years ago. Admittedly, I would have been an extreme cad to do so before breaking it off with Nancy. But I wish I had. That was before I became irrevocably changed in an instant; the line of thought is moot now.

I turn my attention to the real estate database on my computer screen to pull up short sale and foreclosure listings. After a few minutes I hear Gwen blow her nose and finish her beer.

"Feel better?" I ask.

"I'm not a bad person," she says. It sounds like a question.

I look into her tearstained face and somehow she's still beautiful, even though her nose is currently the color of a ripe turnip. "I know what kind of a person you are, Gwen. You've always been good."

I reach out and touch her face. I think what a pair we'd make: a scandalized crybaby looking for a foreclosed home, and a guy whose look only works on Halloween. She puts her hand over mine and nods a big thank you that involves more tears spilling from her eyes.

"Now roll over here and tell me if you'd like to tour any of these houses," I say, taking my hand away from her face and pointing toward the screen. "In order to get the most of your money, you might want to consider buying a house in short sale or foreclosure status."

"Megan's husband said he knows of a nice one in Hidden Pines that's in foreclosure. On Hidden Lakes Drive."

"Okay," I jot that down, in case it meets her criteria.

"Is buying a foreclosure the same as buying a regular house?"

"They are regular houses, but the bank is taking them back because the owner is too far behind on mortgage payments. Sometimes owners don't leave the homes in good shape, and because they tend to be sold very cheaply, the bank isn't usually willing to do repairs like other homeowners would normally negotiate into a deal. Foreclosed and short sale houses are sold in 'as is/where is' condition, which means that the buyer buys at her own risk."

"That sounds scary."

Gwen twists the fringe on her long crocheted sweater and I realize she arrived without a coat. She seems woefully ill prepared for the weather, let alone buying a house.

"Well, I'll be along to help," I assure her.

She looks up at me again, with her red-rimmed eyes. "Are you sure it wouldn't be an imposition? I mean already, it's Friday evening, and instead of being home with your family you're still here at work."

"I don't have a family."

"But you were engaged when I last saw you… Oh my God, did she get hit, too?"

"No, no. Nothing like that. I never got married after all."

I see something pass over Gwen's face that I can't quite read. "I'm sorry, Smith," she says.

"It's okay. When we broke it off Nancy hated me for a while. But after the accident she forgave me, and she and her boyfriend even brought over a casserole when I finally got out of the hospital."

Gwen smiles. She looks incredibly tired, like the entire day has caught up with her at once.

"Where are you staying?" I ask.

"I don't know yet. Is the hotel on Main Street still nice?"

"Well, it has suffered a bit with the slow economy, but I know they'd be glad to have you until you find a place. Let me call Walter Owens, the manager there, to see if he can guarantee you some privacy."

"Walter Owens from school? A few years younger than us?"

I wonder if this is a bad idea. Walter Owens has taken really good care of himself, in the metrosexual sense that stands out in Riveredge, where far more men hunt deer than blow dry their hair. Men around here snigger about a guy who's as into his clothes as Walter, skeptical about anyone who'd arrive for his men's league baseball game freshly shaved and cologned like he's going on a date. The women are divided, I think, but enough of them must like Walter's style because he's known as a lady's man.

"That's him. Or the Holiday Inn just got overhauled…"

"Let's try Walter."

"Did you bring any luggage?" I ask.

Gwen drops her head onto my desk and pounds it a few times. "Damn it! I left my suitcase at the hospital."

I call the Riveredge on Main and get Walter on the line. He seems very excited at the prospect of having Gwen as a guest—too excited for my taste. Like with his primping, he can't seem to stop with enough. "I'll send someone to the hospital to get Gwendolyn's suitcase. I'll put her in the nicest suite we have, and give her a key to the private entrance. Hold on for a minute," he says, and in the background I hear him ask someone to fill her mini fridge. "She's there at your office?" he asks.

"Yes, she's right here."

"Put her on. Please."

Walter Owens is so determined to show his dedication to his new guest that he insists on picking up Gwen. I try to find a reason why I need to drive her there, but I can't.

Gwen and I talk about what kind of a house might work best for her so that I can narrow our options down. We look at a few online until she yawns and rubs her eyes.

"Walter should be here any minute. Meanwhile, I hate to ask you this, but I promised my secretary I'd get your autograph for her. Actually two of them: one for Jessie, and one for her mother."

"I hate signing autographs. Don't you think it's weird?"

"Well, I'm rarely asked for mine." I smile, careful to show her my good side. "It would really help me out if you'd do it. Otherwise I'll have to make forgeries to satisfy her."

Gwen writes: *To Jessie, You're so lucky to work for Smith Walker. Love, Gwendolyn Golden* under her photo in the newspaper. "Is that OK?"

"She'll accuse me of dictating. But what if I was planning to save that? You celebrities are all the same—wanton disregard for the rest of us."

"You were not going to save that!" she says, as if the

idea were beneath me. She yawns again. "Jessie's mother's name is…?"

"Pinky."

"Your secretary has a mother named Pinky?" Gwen asks, her eyes lighting up.

"Yes. Tragic, isn't it?"

"Armand would love it. He'll want a mother named Pinky if I tell him it's possible."

"Jessie might be willing to part with her."

Gwen writes: *To Pinky, you're my favorite color. Love, Gwendolyn Golden* on a sheet of paper she pulled off the printer. I don't mention the fact that Pinky, who can't be a day over a hundred and twelve, is actually more the color of ashy skim milk than her name implies.

"When do you want to go and look at houses?" I ask.

"What works for you?"

"Tomorrow?"

She wrinkles her nose and I see that I overreached. "Tomorrow I'll be at the hospital with my dad all day."

I decide not to go for Sunday; I don't want to scare her off with my enthusiasm. I look through my calendar and see that on Monday I've got back-to-back meetings that must stand. Tuesday I can cancel what I've got planned for the afternoon.

"Tuesday afternoon sound okay?"

"It's a deal," she says, smiling and holding out her hand. I shake it.

She looks down at my scars but doesn't wince. I wonder if she's had special training, in case audience members at interviews are disfigured like me.

"Do your injuries hurt, Smith?" she asks. Most people don't; they generally recoil before pretending they don't see that there's anything wrong at all. Gwen reaches out and takes my hand back. She gently turns it over, studying it. I find that I don't mind somehow.

"Sometimes. In the beginning it was much worse."

"I'm sorry," she says.

"Can I buy you lunch tomorrow?" I ask.

"I can't. I told Megan I'd stay with Dad."

"Right. You said that. It's just so good to see you."

"Maybe I can get away for dinner?" she suggests.

I know Siler's wife Janet is making my favorites tomorrow and I can't cancel. I suppose I could invite Gwen, but that would be incredibly awkward. I never invited her home when I lived in that house as a kid because I knew it was so far beneath her lifestyle. I'm sure it would be even more of a culture shock to bring her there now, after years living in *So Perfect* land.

"Shoot. I've got plans," I say. For a moment I think I see her face fall in disappointment, but then I realize it can't be so— it was more likely relief. She probably only suggested dinner because she's grateful that I've offered to help her, that I'm not fawning all over her, or snapping her picture, or tossing insults. She certainly can't be sad that a broken man she cared for a lifetime ago has dinner plans.

Walter pounds on the lobby doors, here to collect his famous new resident. I get up with my usual speed, which is something akin to a tortoise with a crumpled shell, but Gwen tells me she can find her way.

"So I'll pick you up from the hotel Tuesday at 1:00?" I ask.

"That sounds perfect. Thanks for letting me come tonight, Smith, and for helping me. You're like an island of sanity in the craziest day I've ever had." She leans in for a swift cheek kiss like movie stars give each other, and waves goodbye on her way out the door.

chapter nine

caroline

I barely suppress a shriek when I open my front door.

I feel like one of those poor slobs who answers her doorbell in pajamas, only to be photographed and handed balloons because she's won the sweepstakes. I've always thought that approach was very underhanded, surely someone could call ahead and give a tipoff: *Pssst, throw on a dress and some lipstick because we'll be there in five minutes with cameras.* I know I'm not about to win a jackpot, but this is definitely a case where a little warning would have gone a long way.

"Can we come in?"

I hadn't even noticed the man yet, leaning on his cane. He has a huge scar from his hairline to his chin, which makes his friendly green eyes seem impossible, especially his left one in the middle of the scar. I can't imagine how it could have escaped damage. He smiles and I wonder the same about his teeth.

He hands me a business card. "I'm Smith Walker. I called earlier about showing my client your house. Caroline Penny, right? This is Gwen Golden."

She puts out her hand and I shake it, just like I'd shake anyone else's. It's perfectly normal. The current local media queen is here to look at my soon-to-be-foreclosed-upon home. Of course. This sort of thing happens every day.

"Uh, hi."

I try not to stare too obviously. She's much taller than I am, maybe 5'10. I've only ever seen her made up and dressed to the nines. She's got a bohemian casual look going on tonight that seems to suit her well. Her easygoing, natural beauty is the kind I always envy, because the best I've ever managed is cute—and it never comes easy.

"Do you mind if we show ourselves around?" The man asks after he has slowly made his way inside.

"Go anywhere you like, please. Can I get either of you a drink?"

I followed all the advice in the house selling tips video on Gwendolyn's website. I baked cookies and left a pretty platter of them on the counter. I turned on every light.

"Nothing for me, thanks," Gwendolyn says, smiling openly, as if she's an old friend of mine. This is the weirdest, damndest thing! Gwendolyn Golden is in my house.

"I'll be in the little office here if you have any questions." I point to a tiny formal living room converted to a computer den. I go inside and perch on an overstuffed chair and watch them make their way into the kitchen.

After living in that amazing old mansion in North Carolina, there's no way Gwendolyn Golden could like this house. Maybe she's not looking for herself—of course, why didn't I think of it? She grew up in this town, maybe she's buying a home for an indigent old aunt.

"Oh my God," I hear Gwendolyn say under her breath to the realtor who is dragging his leg as he walks beside her. "It looks like a mini version of the *So Perfect* house!"

I shouldn't have been straining to eavesdrop. Now I know that I've been revealed as a savant to the object of my adoration. Perfect. I feel my face burning with embarrassment as I turn on the computer to try and look busy.

Alas, when I click on the Internet icon it goes to my homepage, which is the *So Perfect* site. In my nervous state, I accidentally click again and the latest video begins to play, with its cute little bars of intro music that ends in Gwendolyn and Armand lightly laughing. I scramble to turn it off and fight the urge to hide.

I breathe deeply to calm down. I have been in perpetual motion all day, so this sudden enforced stillness is jarring to both mind and body. I got the kids off to school, cycled through the laundry, and worked my library shift before coming home to get the house in shape for tonight's viewing. When it was as good as I could get it, I was shocked to discover that I had half an hour to spare before the bus came.

Spare half hours are very rare for me these days, and quiet time for reflection is practically nonexistent, so I decided to follow the advice of my favorite lifestyle guru (who happens to be in my house right now!) and enjoy a quiet tea break. I filled my teakettle and opened a cupboard to see my herbal options, with names that gave me enough optimism in the grocery store aisle to put them in my cart: Calm. Happiness. Hope. Enlightenment.

I drank two cups of Hope before heading outside to await Mr. Marley's bus. I knew from daily experience that he'd pull up alongside the road, put on his safety lights, and open the door for my children to disembark from another day in their school lives. It's still strange to me to think that, moment by moment, they're growing up.

I remember how shocking it was when June first started preschool and began coming home with information that I not only hadn't taught her, but didn't necessarily believe. One of her little friends had said that green was prettier than pink, so June instantly had a new favorite color. One said that PBS Kids shows were for babies, so June's new Clifford backpack embarrassed her. Carrots, always a favorite, were suddenly "pukey."

I still haven't gotten used to the fact that throughout the school year my kids spend more of their sentient moments without me than with me, learning all sorts of things that I'm not privy to, growing not only up, and up, but away. My sister Suzie says it's simply the way it is and there's no use fighting it. I just don't think I'm a trusting enough soul for this process of letting go a little more every day. I want to hold on tight.

The plowed snow was crunchy and deep, and although it was bitter cold this afternoon, I waited outside for the bus to arrive. June knows to lead the twins in through the back door if I'm ever not out there. But the one day I stayed in and watched from the window, James fell down and cried, and I rushed outside anyway. Their days are so long, I never blame them for getting tired and cranky. James and Joy are only in first grade, but they're growing and growing.

After homework came piano practice, and then dinner. Then in a very cheerful voice I said, "We're going to get cleaned up, and you're all going to Aunt Suzie's for a little while."

"It's a school night," eight-year-old June said skeptically.

I smiled big. "I know! But some people are coming to look at the house, and it will be boring for you to stay out of their way. Can you help the twins wipe their faces, honey?"

I tried to keep the tense excitement from my voice, but I feared I was failing. The house has been on the market since I missed the first payment, though I opted to go without a sign to keep a low profile from my sister, the kids, and my neighbors. There aren't many people looking now, and virtually everyone searches online first, so I thought the trade-off was worth it.

Only a handful of potential buyers have walked through. I have almost given up hope of the place selling. The housing market here is terrible; some say it's the worst it has ever been, and anyone with a choice isn't trying to unload property. I don't have a choice, unless I counted asking Blake for help. And I don't.

The bank that holds the mortgage to this house has already started the process of foreclosure. My loan officer explained that if I miraculously get an offer, the bank will have to agree to it in what's called a "short sale." If I don't get an offer, the house will be foreclosed and my credit will be ruined. I say all this in terms of "I," because that's how I feel about it. The house is in Blake's name too, but since I haven't seen him around here for the past six months, I don't think in terms of "we" anymore.

"I'm not moving!" James yelled while June wiped his face with a wet paper towel. I wished I hadn't fed them spaghetti, there was a layer of sauce all over the table.

I wondered if I made the right choice explaining the basics to the kids over dinner. I thought it would be better to let them absorb it in stages instead of springing it on them all at once when we're forced to move out.

"We *have* to move," Joy reminded her twin. "We're being foretold so we have to move no matter what. Right, Mom?" Joy wiped her own mouth.

"That's right. But don't worry," I told them. I say that phrase to my children almost constantly these days. "We'll move somewhere nearby, and maybe at first it won't be perfect, but I'll make it really great for us."

"Within the school district?" June asked with panic in her voice.

I stopped cleaning the table and turned to face her. "I *promise*, June."

I know how hard it was for her when Blake left. I know how much she needs to trust the things that remain, like the familiarity of her friends and teachers. I won't tear her away from all that. June gave me her brave smile and kept the twins on task as they put their shoes and coats on and headed for the door.

"Aunt Suzie knows we're coming?" June asked.

Suzie is ten years my senior and has always been a more conscientious mom to me than our real one. She moved here to be close to me and the kids, and I'm afraid to imagine what would happen to us without her.

"Of course, honey," I replied.

I have never let the children go anywhere without careful thought and planning. Sending them four houses down to my sister's is as far as I will ever let them go alone while they're so small. It made me sad to hear my eight-year-old daughter imply that I might send them off into the night without a warm and welcoming destination planned.

Sometimes I feel that although I've been banking up love, and care, and sleepless nights, and endless hours of nursing and rocking each of them, there's still not a single dime in my Mom account that I can draw on. Motherhood is *for deposit only*. I guess that's as it should be while the children are young, but if they try to put me in a home someday, I swear I will not go quietly.

"Please bring these to Aunt Suzie," I said, handing June a box of the warm cookies I had just baked so the house would smell lovely. "But don't let Uncle Dan gobble them all up. Tell him I said that he has to share."

Joy and James giggled. June held the box like it was full of fine china.

"If you drop it, that's OK. Cookies are yummy no matter if they're whole or broken," I told her.

June nodded but didn't relax her grip.

"I'll be there soon," I said as they trudged out. I watched them march along the sidewalk in their snow boots until they entered Suzie's house.

I hear footsteps above me, along with muffled voices. I can't quite believe that Gwendolyn Golden is standing in my master bathroom! I hear the thunk of a cane overhead followed by a sliding sound. I remember noting that the realtor had nice shoes that appeared to be evenly worn, and I wonder how he manages that. It's strange to think of carrying your damage on the outside where everyone can see it.

Soon I hear footsteps coming back down the stairs. I wait for a long time while a hushed conversation takes place in the kitchen. No one has gone through the house in weeks. There are so many homes for sale, and so few buyers, that I've been trying to reconcile myself to either losing this house or going to Blake for help. I'm so torn about it. On one hand, it's his house, too, and his credit along with mine that will be ruined. On the other hand, I picture him and his "colleague" Francine enjoying the sunny weather in Spain during breaks from their long-term project abroad, and I think that having his credit ruined would be a drop in the bucket compared to the flood he deserves.

I close my eyes and try to breathe evenly. I don't want to think of how awful it will be when Gwendolyn and her realtor thank me and leave. How I'll have to smile and say it was my pleasure, and then smile bigger when I tell the kids there's nothing to worry about, that the right buyer might still come along in time.

When I don't think I can stand the suspense a moment

longer, I hear the thunk-shuffle down the hall and look up to see Gwendolyn Golden already in the doorway.

I burst into Suzie's house without knocking. The kids look up in shock, like something awful is going to happen, suspended in mid-chew. James has milk dripping down his face and Joy somehow managed to get chocolate on her forehead.

Then they re-animate, each smiling a gorgeous smile of relief, and I realize that they haven't seen me truly happy in a long time.

"We have a good offer!"

Suzie hugs me, and I feel an overwhelming sense of gratefulness.

"It's enough for the bank to approve," I say, testing the words. "I won't lose my credit. We may even be able to buy a smaller place that needs some work, maybe right here in this neighborhood."

June smiles and it looks so genuine that I feel tears on my cheeks.

I suddenly understand how terrified I have been for the past six months since Blake left. I knew I was angry, I knew I was disappointed, but I hadn't allowed myself to face how truly *scared* I've been.

"What's wrong, Mom?" James asks, looking up at me. He reaches out his napkin to dry my tears.

"Don't worry. These are happy tears, honey. Don't worry!"

My tears mix with laughter as I scoop him up into my arms and dance him around Suzie's kitchen.

chapter ten

armand

I haven't seen Gwendolyn in two whole weeks, not since I left for what was supposed to be a long, fun weekend in New York City. I'm on my way to her now because I just can't stand it anymore—I miss the poor kid something fierce! I also need to explain to her what Trey's been cooking up, with me stewing right in the middle of the pot, making me the main course at his big old banquet.

Trey's focus groups have done an about-face, not just about my face, but about my lisp, my walk, my hair, and everything else about me. They seem to think I'm delicious now—even better alone than I was with Gwendolyn. She's been taking all the tabloid guff about our faking it. I don't think that's very fair... but then again, I was the mastermind chef, decorator, and gardener, and I have to admit it's kind of nice that people are beginning to know it.

I just wish there could be a good guy without a fall guy! If I don't get Gwendolyn's blessing I might have to stop poking around in the ashes of our former empire with Trey. I hope she says I'm free to spread my wings and fly out like a phoenix. If she doesn't, I don't know what I'll do.

My plane lands hard on the runway and I look out my little rectangle of window to see flat land for miles.

I didn't realize anywhere on earth could be so blessed cold. The weather here is drizzle-nasty, and the sky's so gray it almost matches my roots. Ugly billboards line the pot-holed pavement, and they only seem to point further into nowhere. I shouldn't keep on complaining this way—my mama always said that saying mean things would sprout thorns from my tongue.

But is it mean to notice that the houses along this sad, flat highway look like dentist offices built in the 1970's? They're all single-storied and flat-roofed, like whimsy is a sin. Some have brick the color of blah, others wear bland beige siding in desperate need of a good old-fashioned power washing. Every car I see is dirty with age and road salt. The few patches of dead grass that show through the snow look like bald spots on the heads of sad old farmers with their pants pulled up to their armpits.

Only twenty minutes on the ground and I'm already depressed!

I follow the directions of my GPS toward Gwendolyn's future home, where I said I'd meet her. I wish Gypsy, my dependable little electronic friend, had different voices that I could switch out, like Donald Duck, or Blake Shelton, or the Queen Mother. Maybe it does and I just don't know how to work it. I make a few turns like I'm told, and either it's starting to get prettier outside my window or I'm growing accustomed to how things appear under thick cloud cover. I snailpace through the cute downtown that hugs the river, past the Victorians in a respectable row that are looking tidy even in the dull weather, proving times aren't so tough here that the treasures are being let go.

I speed up again once I'm out of the town limits. A few more miles and I turn down the street my Gypsy tells me to. The earth is very flat here, and besides the man-made buildings and haphazard landscaping, there's not much to look at. The village I passed through had some history and charm to it, and I liked how it was snuggled up cozy with the river. I bet after a fresh layer of snowfall to hide the muddiness, it would make a sweet picture.

Contrast that to the subdivision I'm being led into now, like a modern-day Hansel minus the retro lederhosen. Hidden Pines looks like it isn't comfortable with itself yet. The landscape plants haven't grown into their full potential, and the gardens don't seem to have been designed at all. The houses aren't new enough to still be shiny, fresh, and innocent, but they're not old enough to have earned themselves some character either. It's not a place I'd ever choose to live, that's for sure. I'll have to trust that Gypsy is more reliable than breadcrumbs and will get me back to civilization okay.

Trey had suggested a suburban *So Perfect* house at first, but I'm allergic to subdivisions. Even the crazy expensive ones where each house sits on two acres with its own Tuscan style swimming pool out back, circular driveway out front, and pillars strewn *everywhere* make me break out in hives. The sameness, the blatantly trying so hard to fit in…

It brings to mind a garden I designed five years ago for a suburban woman named Jen. I thought Jen was funny and interesting, in the way that the first person you meet from an exotic country seems novel, carrying all the charm and newness of their type. I chuckled at the snide remarks she made about her life in the 'burbs, which were very witty in a Dorothy Parker sort of way. Jen was a forty-something woman of leisure who'd set aside her career to raise her kids then decided she'd never pick it back up again.

Jen acted like she was my gal pal while we worked together. She loved my designs, and bless her heart, she never raised an over-plucked eyebrow at the costs. She kept telling me about a hairdresser friend of hers named Carl, saying he just couldn't seem to find the right guy. It was clear she suspected I was gay, but I didn't confirm or deny. Not everyone can be trusted, and I didn't want to be Jen's gay mascot or whatever it was she wanted me to be. I wish it were true that I'm out all the time and not just on a limited case-by-case basis, but it has never been that way for me.

Though I'm sure they're everywhere, I had never met a woman like Jen before. Getting to know her was like how you feel when you first get a special car—it seems like you're the only person who has it. But soon you start noticing them all over, and eventually you find yourself walking up to the wrong one at the supermarket.

One day I accepted Jen's invitation to lunch with her friends. When we got to the table I couldn't help myself, I let out a small gasp and bit my lip to stop a fit of giggles, the likes of which used to come over me in church and I'd always get whipped for afterwards. The three women sitting there all looked like Jen. A *lot* like Jen. I got myself under control and joined them in a midday glass of wine before we ordered. I felt like an undercover reporter, because I just *had* to know what in heaven's name was going on with those ladies! Were they being mass-produced by some middle-aged executive with a straight blonde hair fetish, a penchant for Botox, and an obsession with suspiciously perky boobs?

One of the ladies said she'd just come from Carl's, and they all gushed about him for a while, making it clear he was the stylist to all. I think the chitchat was for my benefit because it was about Carl's love life and how he just had to find the right guy. I kind of wanted to meet this Carl then, to find out if he knew that four of his clients regularly hung out together, and to ask him if it wasn't a professional ethics breach to give them all the same hair color and cuts.

It was soon clear that unless Carl listened to his iPod on maximum volume while he styled, he knew the women hung out, along with details about their neighbors, husbands, sex lives, mothers-in-law…you name it. I decided to cut the poor guy some slack about his ethical lapses, figuring he had to cope somehow.

I turn deeper into the subdivision only because Gypsy tells me to. If not for the street names I'm afraid I could get lost in here forever, like a spooky haunted corn maze on Halloween. It makes me sad to think of Gwendolyn stuck in this wasteland. But I remind myself that as long as there's good light and room for a canvas, Gwendolyn will probably be fine just about anywhere. My cell phone rings and I click it on and try to sound depressed when I see it's her. "Oh. Hi."

"Hey! Where are you?"

"I'm sorry. I missed my plane and I just can't get another flight…"

"Is that you coming up the street?" she asks, completely

over the top of what I'm saying. I see a tall, skinny, crazy lady standing in the rain outside of a pretty white bungalow, waving like the house is on fire. I click off my phone. She's beside my car before I can open the door. When I step out, she flings herself into my arms.

"How did you know it was me in this sorry little rental car? You could have just flagged down a serial nutjob!"

"I knew your plane landed on time and I've been watching. This is a dead end street and barely anyone comes down here."

Gwendolyn's smile is huge, she looks toothier than usual, and her eyes seem bigger. These aren't pluses. As she leads the way up the sidewalk, I notice her pants are saggy in the bottom. I know for a fact those jeans fit her cute just two weeks ago.

"You're too thin."

"No one cooks for me," she says as she opens the door.

"You still have to eat."

She gestures for me to go ahead of her. "This is it."

After a quick jog around the main floor, I decide that the current owner of this house is hands-down the best student I've ever had. Her dynamic furniture placement, her playful mixture of colors and textures, her ability to toss whimsical elements into an otherwise eclectic design... By the time I catch up with Gwendolyn again I have to ask, "Lord in heaven, where's my mini-me hiding?"

"She left so I could show you through."

"Didn't she want to meet me? I must be her idol."

Gwendolyn looks at me patiently, and I'm reminded why I've been missing her so much... She puts up with me.

"I bet Caroline would have liked to meet you, but she's working on her new place."

"Well, I have to meet her," I say.

Gwendolyn frowns like she's confused. I flash way back to her piecrust attempts, when she was determined to learn every recipe so she wouldn't feel like a fraud. I think that phase lasted a month, ending in part because Trey threatened to make her pay for kitchen fire damage.

"Why do you want to meet her?" she asks.

"Wouldn't you want to meet a painter who is similar to you, but maybe even better in some ways? Wouldn't you want to talk about style and philosophy? Maybe learn a little?"

"I told Caroline I'd call her when we're done anyway, so I'll tell her you want to meet. Now can you look around and give me some advice?"

I take off my leather jacket and hang it over the back of a friendly red wicker chair with a retro-floral cushion. "Have you measured the rooms yet?" I ask. "Have you thought about colors? Do you have a furniture budget in mind?"

I know Gwendolyn doesn't have answers; the little vertical line between her eyes says she's worried and in over her head. Her face lightens suddenly.

"Caroline left some stuff on the counter when I told her you were coming."

I follow Gwendolyn into the kitchen and see a neat little kit containing a paint deck, tape measure, pencil, and pad of paper. It's exactly the decorating kit we advised on a video once! I'm feeling soft toward this Caroline. It's not only because she has such good taste in designers and follows advice so well, I also saw a photo display in the hall and noticed that she and her kids couldn't be more adorable.

"You said this place was being foreclosed?" I ask.

"Yeah. Sad, huh? Apparently Caroline's husband left and she couldn't hold on to it."

"You know what else is sad? How much work is needed before you can move in! When Caroline takes her stuff out, this place won't be recognizable." I put my hands on my hips in what I know is a stereotypical gay stance. I can try this sort of thing out on Gwendolyn and she won't judge me.

"Is this new?" she asks, mirroring my posture.

I've been living in don't ask/don't tell hell for the past two weeks—ever since Norman and I made the news. I honestly don't know how to act! People used to think of me as the straight husband who gave the thumbs-up sign to Gwendolyn when I tasted a *So Perfect* recipe. The guy who kept his lispy mouth shut while he carved her turkey, or stacked her firewood, or put up her twelve foot high Christmas tree in the family room.

"Does it work for me?"

She tilts her head and seems to really consider the matter.

"If you like it, I like it."

I wish I knew if I liked it! I feel like a gay teenager probably feels, if he isn't terrified into denial by constant threats of fire and brimstone and gets to be freely gay in the world. Just because Trey now says the focus groups are fine with my alternative lifestyle (which is what he calls it), that doesn't mean a certain heavyset woman in Praiseville agrees. I am so confused! I should have been figuring this stuff out when I was fifteen.

"What can I do?" Gwendolyn asks, picking up the tape measure. She looks hopeful and trusting. I am suddenly very sad for her. I strongly suspect she bought this house because it was decorated like the *So Perfect* one, as much as was possible for a house less than a quarter the size, with none of the architectural grandeur. Gwendolyn appears to have no idea that when the furnishings and accessories are gone, it won't be special anymore.

"Do you own anything? Like rugs or lamps or dishes?" I ask, though I fear the answer is no. I didn't have to incorporate any of her personal things into the Scenic house except mementos and art supplies.

"Not really."

I know from her photo albums that Gwendolyn grew up quite wealthy. I wonder how it is that a twenty-nine year old woman has accumulated nothing on her journey through life except painting paraphernalia.

I consider talking her into going out for drinks before dinner and just pretending I never saw this doomed project. She's counting on me, though. So few people have ever depended on me, as a friend not a hired genius; it feels novel and I don't want to ruin it. Plus I need to be on her good side for the conversation we've got to have.

I take the tape measure from her hands and begin measuring the breakfast nook. "OK, so you're starting from scratch. How much can you spend?"

She shrugs.

I let the tape recoil back into its case with a loud snap and stare at her. I'm at a total loss for how a smart girl like Gwendolyn is such a total dimwit when it comes to basic practicalities.

"You think I'm hopeless," she says, not like she's mad or sad, but just stating it.

I shake my head and chuckle. She knows me way too well! I had no siblings. Friendships were awkward for me because girls didn't understand why I didn't want to kiss them, and when guys suspected that I did, it became touchy. Gwendolyn and I hit it off from the first day. She says I picked her, that she was the one on approval and I had all the power to say yea or nay. Really though, the fact that she seemed to trust my judgment and accept me with no questions asked made it easy. I liked her art, too, but aside from the pieces she creates in a crazy fog, I bet there are lots of painters who can do better. I think I picked Gwendolyn because she wanted me to, and because she let me.

"I think you're smart about a lot of things," I say.

She puts her hand in mine and gives me that understanding smile of hers. "But stupid when it comes to keeping house?"

"I'm just sayin'."

We both laugh a little and it's a relief to see we're still a team. A dysfunctional one, there's no question about that, but a loving one, too. When the story first broke, I thought that for as long as anyone still cared, I'd be known as the guy who tarnished the Golden image. For whatever fickle reason though, the story hasn't fizzled, but has picked up tabloid steam. While I seem to be weathering the public opinion storm, Gwendolyn has been getting pelted.

"Have you read any of the stories about us?" I ask.

"No! I can't believe anyone cares."

I thought at first Gwendolyn protested too much, that she really liked the attention we got when we went to dinner or the movies, or when the horse-and-buggy city tour stopped in front of the Grand Dame and people took photographs and strained to catch glimpses of us. I loved that part. I wished I could be myself, I wished I could take credit for my work, but even the deflected adulation was pretty great. Gwendolyn never warmed to it, though. Maybe people had always looked up to her and treated her nice and that's why it wasn't as big a deal to her as it was to me.

"I guess it's kind of flattering that we're not already forgotten."

"I wish we were! My dad tells me about all the snarky little things he's read or seen on television. He and my sister are mortified, so that sucks."

"How's your dad health-wise?"

"He's back at home in his normal routine. His tests came out fine and they tweaked his medicine and told him to get more exercise. I spend most of my days at his place. He let me set up an easel in his spare bedroom, which has south-facing windows."

"And how's your sister?"

"She's a bitch, same as ever."

"Do you have any friends?"

"My realtor has been wonderful. He let me store my stuff from the Scenic house in one of his buildings until I move in here."

Gwendolyn blushes a little, and I know she must've heard about Trey's publicity stunt. After a weeklong lull in the story, he called Stuart Bolder in and made a big production out of sending her possessions off in a U-Haul. Stuart implied that Gwendolyn was a diva with a shoe closet like Paris Hilton's, but I know she usually dresses like she's dressed now: jeans, a fitted t-shirt (in this case it's robin's egg blue and washes out her hazel eyes to an eerie shade of pale), a long crocheted cardigan sweater she takes off and misplaces when she's warm, and cowboy boots. Even in summer. I tried to coax Gwen out of her wardrobe rut for four years running so I know she doesn't own any clothes besides the laundry list of things I mentioned. I'm guessing they kept the things she wore on camera. I think Trey packed Gwendolyn's truck half full of empty boxes to make the poor kid look worse than everyone thinks she is.

I look at her sweet face and her crumpled hair, which is suffering mightily from two weeks of neglect. She reaches around my waist and hooks her thumb in my belt hoop in that winning way audiences loved during television spots.

"So, what will I need to make this house a home?"

"A magic wand."

"I have better than that. I have you!"

I look around nervously and check my watch. "Seriously now, what can you spend?"

"Until Trey lets me cash out my stock options, I've got to be on a strict budget. I should only take about $5,000 to get moved in."

I bite my lip and think for a minute. "We can get you a nice sofa, maybe a coffee table, and a footstool, if I really stretch it."

She widens her eyes in surprise and I have to look away.

"Is that really all?"

"If I'm doing the buying," I tell her honestly. I sweep my eyes around the kitchen. "There are almost certainly cheaper ways to go, though. Maybe Caroline can help you?"

I know that it's one thing to have a staff and an unlimited credit card, and quite another to make magic on a budget. The lady who put this house together did what she could with what she had, and the effect is sweet and homey. She paired a newish sofa with mismatched old leather club chairs she probably picked up in a thrift store, and they look like they're having a jolly old conversation together in the family room. She flanked four matching wooden chairs around the dining table and then punched it up with contrasting brightly-painted chairs on either end. She has a delightful sense of color, texture, proportion, and whimsy. Every edge is softened into something at once so chic and so earnest.

"I think she has her hands full already. But thanks for telling it to me straight," Gwendolyn says.

Together we walk through the house and make some rough measurements. I suggest a few places where Gwendolyn might hang her favorite paintings, and what furniture pieces would look nice where, if she can find inexpensive sources or another fifty grand.

As I go from room to room, I try to put my finger on why Caroline's house looks so fresh to me. It takes me a little while to place it, but when I do, I see it everywhere—it's evidence of her kids. They're infused into each room of the house. School calendars are pinned on to a bulletin board beside clever wall pockets holding schoolwork. A computer nook makes smart use of the tiny formal living room. Lively children's artwork has been taped up to brighten the dull white door to the laundry room from the kitchen, and on the breakfast room windows to conceal an otherwise boring view of the side of a neighbor's house. The way she made room for her kids' work and play just seems effortless, and beautiful.

"My mother threw away all my art. She never thought it was any good," Gwendolyn says as she admires the handiwork of Caroline's kids.

"She was probably just a neat freak," I say.

Gwendolyn's sad smile says I'm full of crap.

"Are you complaining to *me* about mothers?" I ask. We both laugh a little.

"I wish I could be more helpful," I say after we've walked through the house and Gwendolyn has scratched down notes as I talked and motioned. She said she's going to leave an upstairs bedroom empty to use as a studio, because it's the only room with adequate natural light. I agree that sounds like a swell idea, but I don't mention that most of her house is likely to be empty for a good long while.

"You were a huge help!" she says, frowning down at her notes that are in such a jumble I doubt she can even read them. I notice she sketched an easel in the upstairs room, but that's the only thing she drew.

"I wish I could make you dinner, you look half starved. Are there any five star restaurants around here?"

"I either eat with my dad or order room service at the hotel where I'm staying. When I move in here I'll be able to cook," she looks down at the scuffed toes of her cowboy boots.

"Why don't we go see and be seen, and photographed, so that it's clear to the world we're best friends, no matter how anyone tries to spin it?"

"I'd rather keep lying low," she says.

"Take it from the infamous Armand Leopold—you can't hide out forever." I half spin, thinking how ironic it is that my bible-thumping mother gave me such a fabulous gay name. I raise my eyebrows at Gwen about my move, but she shrugs her shoulders as if to say the question of whether to half spin or not to half spin is really up to me.

"My dad said you're doing an interview next week? He saw a commercial for it," she says, cutting to the chase.

"That's why I wanted to see you so bad," I confess. "I wanted you to know I don't have a choice in the matter. Trey's been trying to get me to do it from day one, remember? He pointed out contract language until my eyes glazed over. He threatened to sue if I didn't agree to talk." That's technically true, though I didn't argue too hard either, once I heard what the focus groups said.

"My dad said it looks like they're really hyping it."

I know this. I know the ads make it look like I'm the good guy and she's a selfish diva. "You know I love you," I tell her.

"I trust you," she says.

My stomach sinks because I see she means it.

Gwendolyn points out the window during our drive away from her place in my rental car.

"This is the house Caroline is moving to. Smith told me when he dropped me off earlier."

"Smith?" I ask and notice that Gwendolyn blushes. To my knowledge, she hasn't so much as kissed a boy in the time I've known her.

"It's a long story," she says.

I put my foot on the brake so we lurch a little. "Is Caroline there now?"

"That's her car. I forgot to call to say we're done at her house."

Gwendolyn pulls out her cell phone but I park in the driveway instead. I really want to meet this Caroline woman. "Let's tell her in person," I say, getting out.

Gwendolyn seems very reluctant. "I don't want to impose. I told her I'd call…"

By the time she finishes her argument I'm already ringing the bell. Through the dirty little window in the front door I see an ugly, filthy house. Everything about it is nasty. Finally a woman wearing rubber gloves, a surgical mask, and carrying a half filled garbage bag appears.

"Caroline Penny?"

She pulls down her mask. She looks exhausted, dirty, and life-threateningly embarrassed. I guess I get it; I certainly wouldn't want my idol to see me in a similar situation.

"I didn't expect to meet you," she says, frowning at her rubber gloves.

I flash my winning smile. "I just toured your house with Gwendolyn."

She bites her lip. "I suppose I seem pretty foolish, following all your instructions to the letter like I don't have any ideas of my own."

"No! I think you're brilliant! You're *my* new idol." I flop my hand and instantly regret it. I peek over to Gwendolyn and she averts her eyes.

"Right," Caroline whispers.

"We're done at your house, Caroline," Gwendolyn says apologetically. "Thanks for letting us go through."

"I'd love to talk design with you," I say cheerfully, because the ladies seem to think this conversation is over and I'm not ready for it to end.

"I can't. I've got my hands full."

And she does. Literally. Full of nasty stuff in a garbage bag that I can smell from six feet away. "Tomorrow? I'm in town until late afternoon," I say.

"I'm sorry, but I've got to spend every spare minute on this house. We move in three weeks from now."

"Three weeks?" I say in a shocked tone that I regret even more than the hand flop. Caroline looks like she might burst into tears. She steps in front of me so that I can't peek beyond her to see what she's up against.

"Three weeks," she says like she actually thinks it's possible. She pulls up her mask, slips back inside, and shuts the door.

"See why I'm thin?" Gwendolyn asks over a cardboard turkey and brick biscuit dinner in her hotel room. I don't know how she can stand living in this small suite with no view whatsoever. She's been here for two weeks already, with another three to go before she closes on her new place and moves in. I'd go nuts.

"Does the hotel manager bring up everyone's room service, or does he just do it for you?" I watch her closely to see if the obvious crush the hotel guy has on her is mutual, or if she has even noticed it.

She wrinkles her nose. "I think he just does it for me."

"He's cute!"

"Is he?" she asks, like she honestly hasn't noticed. She lowers her voice to a whisper. "He keeps bringing me flowers and asking me out…" She leans in so she's whispering right in my ear, "Sometimes when I peek through the peep hole he's standing out in the hall staring at the door."

"He's like the dude in *My Fair Lady* waiting in the street for Eliza Doolittle!" I say.

"Shhhh!" Gwen covers up my mouth and we huddle together, giggling as quietly as we can, as if he's out there right now.

"But he *is* cute," I say after I have recovered enough so that Gwen lets me have my mouth back. "Are you tempted?"

"Nah. I went to school with Walter and he was always a nice guy. But he's not my type."

"What is your type?"

She shrugs and blushes. I love the way she blushes; she gets this rosy pink color that spreads from her cheeks down her neck.

"Does it feel good to be out?" she asks, changing the subject.

I pretend I didn't hear her as I divide the rest of the wine between our glasses. This is the second bottle tonight, which makes it only the tenth or twelfth bottle we've ever shared in all the time we've known each other.

"So, does it?" she asks again.

I sigh heavily before I look over to find her staring slightly cross-eyed with drunkenness. I giggle so hard I go from sitting in the chair to lying on the floor, somehow managing to keep my glass upright. I lift my head and finish the drink in one swill.

"Okay," I tell her seriously. "If you really must know, I'm not exactly 'out.'"

"Uh, yeah you are." She moves from her chair to the floor beside me.

"No. Not really."

"How not? Your picture was in the paper making out with a man! It's been on television. It led to us losing our jobs and getting kicked out of our home. How can you say you're not out?"

I resent that she's suddenly so clear and lucid. "Well, whenever I'm asked if I'm gay, I don't answer."

She frowns at me like I've let her down, like I've let myself down. "You're trying to be coy?"

Actually, I'm trying to keep my mother from being so ashamed she calls me *deviant* again. I wish it were coyness, because that's better than what it really is: cowardice, plain and simple. I'm too scared to say who I am. I'm not proud that I'm a chicken, but I know Gwendolyn will let me get away with it. She lets me get away with everything.

"I aspire to coy. Really, I'm just plain scared."

"You're not just plain anything. You're complicated and talented and brave. I think you're perfect," she says before promptly curling up with my leg for a pillow and falling asleep.

I pet her ratty hair and make a mental note to send her some baked goods. She needs to put some meat on her scrawny bones.

I watch her face while she sleeps and think how sweet it was of her to say I'm perfect. I don't think anyone has ever said that to me before. Maybe it's why I liked the name *So Perfect*, because that's what I've been chasing all this time. I probably should have gone for something more realistic, like *Good Enough*.

chapter eleven

gwendolyn

I run for the phone and try to dial with shaking fingers.

"What are you doing?" my dad demands. I'm terrified he's going to have a heart attack.

"I'm calling 911!"

"Give me that phone!" He turns his vermilion face away from Armand on the television screen, leans up from his recliner, and snatches the phone away from me. Clutching it tight, he falls back into his seat.

I watch my dad watch Armand. I hold my breath. While I hate the interview too, at least I'm not going ballistic. I'm not even really angry as much as I am hurt. My face has been hot with embarrassment from the very first question that Stuart Bolder asked. *The first thing our viewers want to know is, how long did it usually take Gwendolyn to memorize your lessons well enough to pass them off as her own?*

The interview is being conducted in the *So Perfect* house, so I know that Trey is somewhere in the background, orchestrating it all like a smug puppeteer. The large dining room is set up with seating for fifty; Stuart and Armand are in the adjacent family room on the leather sofa, on a raised platform for the occasion, and turned to face the audience.

Armand laughed at the first question and shook his head. The dining room crowd clapped and nodded, as if they understood Stuart to mean it must've taken a loooong time to teach that Gwendolyn Golden boob anything at all.

"I told you you're the fall guy, Dedo! You've lost the fight."

My dad's fist is clenched around the remote; his knuckles are white.

"I'm not in a fight," I mumble.

My dad has tried to share what the tabloids have said about me all along, and I've tried not to listen. I'm only watching this interview because he turned it on. I've only kept watching because he won't let me turn it off.

Stuart asks more questions that I can tell were fed to him. *Is it true that Gwendolyn set the kitchen on fire three times? Is there a more hopeless cook and clueless decorator in existence than Gwendolyn Golden?*

If Armand were here in this room teasing me, I would laugh along with him. I've always known the life we lived was more than a little absurd. Armand isn't here, though, and I'm not in on the joke. I am the joke.

My dad is definitely not laughing. If he wasn't apoplectic, and if Armand wasn't mocking me on television, I'd be able to enjoy watching my old partner in crime. His on-camera presence is impressive and I know for a fact the old focus groups had it wrong when they said I was more likable. Armand's occasional slight lisp is working for him. He looks gorgeous in a heather blue sweater and jeans, his roots neatly touched up and his hair mussed to perfection. His voice is at once confident and confidential, and the way he laughs makes it seem like he's sharing a private joke. Which I suppose he is.

"Have you seen your old partner since you were outed as a fake couple?" Stuart asks, smiling in a way that's hard to read. Armand looks a bit nervous.

"Actually I visited her last week. We're joshing her in good fun here tonight, but she's a wonderful kid and a good friend."

"Why would you call her a kid?" Stuart leans closer to Armand, but not too close, like he's drawn an invisible line he knows he shouldn't cross.

"I don't know. I guess she's a little helpless about some things," Armand says, still apparently trying to keep things light.

"Like?" Stuart asks.

"Like feeding and watering herself, for example. Making her bed, cleaning up her messes, paying her bills. Anything besides painting." Armand laughs lightly.

My dad growls beside me.

"At least she's a great painter, right?" Stuart asks in a loaded sort of way.

I hold my breath and stare at Armand. He can tease me all day long about my inability to cook, the fact that I'm a slob, my distrust of magnifying mirrors, or my boredom with fashion trends, really almost anything at all. If he disses my work, though, I'm going to be seriously hurt.

"Right?" Stuart asks again.

"Well, look here," Armand points to something on the sofa cushion beside him, "there's turquoise paint on my distressed leather! Gwendolyn spreads paint all over the house because she's as careless as a five-year-old. She ruined gold silk curtains in her bedroom by somehow getting magenta paint all over them! On a ten foot high window? Those drapes, with their blackout linings and beaded tassels, were worth a thousand dollars!"

"Does she paint well, on canvas?" Stuart asks.

Armand shrugs his shoulders. "Let's just say her pictures look nice on house wares, but I doubt she'll ever have her own wall at the Met."

As Stuart Bolder breaks for a commercial, a montage of images fills the screen in succession, including the photo of Armand and his one night stand that started it all, street side shots of the Grand Dame, me looking my best in an early catalog photo, and entering the hospital here in Riveredge looking my worst.

I don't see any of it completely clearly. I only half see and half remember the images because my vision is blurred by tears. *Let's just say?* Well, screw him! Armand has told me a million times that he loves my work. I wonder what else he has lied about.

I shut off the TV despite my dad's protests.

"Can you believe your own husband turned on you like that, Gwen-o?"

"You know he isn't really my husband," I say after blowing my nose.

"Still!"

My dad's outrage seems to lessen when a few minutes have gone by. "Did you really set the kitchen on fire three times?"

I sigh. "Four."

At first I really tried to learn to make all the recipes. It felt wrong pretending to be competent at unfamiliar tasks, but Trey said he hadn't hired me to burn the house down. Armand could teach me what I needed to know, when I needed to know it. I should just paint, relax, and maybe lose five pounds before the next catalog shoot—or gain five—the main point being that I was never quite right.

"Your mom was a great cook. She tried to teach you a few times, too, remember?"

It felt like a boxing match whenever my mother and I tried to do something together. We'd rush in and tangle for a few minutes, then go cool off in our respective corners, Megan in my mother's, Dad in mine. I remember a thousand screaming matches and slammed doors.

"Megan learned her way around the kitchen. But you and your mom were too much alike to get along," he says.

I look up at him. "If we were so much alike, why did she hate me?"

"*Hate* you?" he asks, like I have just asked the stupidest question in the history of the entire world.

I don't retreat though, because I know she hated me. I was there. I stare back at him with my arms folded.

He shakes his head like I'm an entire swarm of gnats buzzing around his head, bugging the crap out of him. "She didn't hate you! She loved you girls. Maybe she thought it was a weakness to show it… Trust me, you would've thought she was downright warm if you'd ever gotten to know *her* mother. Now *that* woman was a Grade-A bitch."

I sniff dismissively, like I might if he were defending a serial killer by telling me about the guy's sad childhood. As if blame can just be batted around like a balloon forever, never to land.

"Your mom wasn't a patient woman, I'll concede that. But if you remember, as hard as she was on you girls, she was ten times harder on herself."

I know this is true. My mother would rip out five hours' worth of precise quilting stitches if she discovered she'd made an error that no one, not even with a magnifying glass, would ever notice. She'd throw away a batch of cookies if the color wasn't absolutely perfect. I'd have to sneak some from the garbage can when she huffed out to the patio for a cigarette.

My mother wanted precision and perfection in herself and everything around her. Maybe that's why I was drawn to art: she couldn't prove that what I painted was wrong. She might not find it to her liking, in fact she never complimented any of my work that I can recall. But she couldn't point to how, exactly, it failed to measure up, like she did with everything else about me.

I'm shook up, embarrassed, and hurt by the things Armand said. I don't want to go back to the hotel, though. It doesn't seem at all like home, and I'm afraid Walter the manager will try to comfort me. When I first checked in, he asked what my favorite color was and I just randomly picked lavender because I love so many colors I don't really have a favorite. Ever since then, each time I come back to my room there is something new and lavender there. It started with a bouquet of actual lavenders, then the bed linens, and towels, and shower curtain... Everyone says that Walter's so sweet, but I'm starting to wonder, what is the difference between an admirer and a stalker?

I don't feel like painting in my dad's spare room either. Not right now. I walk to his kitchen with hunched shoulders to fetch him a beer. I don't trust my dad to keep the TV off unless I babysit him, and I don't want him to get upset watching the rest of Armand's interview.

I spend some time neatening the condo kitchen. I unload the dishwasher, which is full of the same dishes I used as a kid. The canisters, silverware, salt and pepper shakers and pans— everything here used to be in our big house on Park Street.

I put in a load of laundry, fold the towels from the dryer and put them in my dad's bathroom. I've been keeping his place up since he got home from the hospital. His stint there was so short that he never missed a single Wednesday morning billiards tournament at the club house, or a Friday evening poker game. Last week I popped in on the latter.

I was surprised to see the exact same group of men I remembered from my dad's poker games during my childhood. If I happened to wander in back then, the men razzed me about boys, or my performance in a volleyball game, or an art award I had won. At the senior clubhouse they picked up where they had left off, teasing me about being on TV.

Since the men aren't allowed to smoke in the clubhouse, unlit cigars hung from their mouths as they played. Some of them live in the senior community, and some drive out for the games. I had a sense of continuity and rightness, seeing them all together, knowing they'd been together so many times over the years, throughout so many changes in their lives. I kissed each one on the cheek as I left. *Can I have your autograph?* Ed Hurley teased.

I had almost forgotten what it was like to live in a small town. I have known so many people here, for so long, I've found unexpected comfort in recognizing an approaching face as someone I actually know, not someone who thinks they know me because they've seen my photographs or watched me on television. I have run into Smith's mom at the clubhouse a few times already, because she lives here in the senior community. Each time she has greeted me exactly like she always had. I'm grateful for the normalcy of simply saying hello to an old acquaintance, as if I'm as entitled to such moments as everyone else.

"It's nice to have you around, Lynny. Your sister's always in such a damn hurry, but you don't mind hanging out with your old man," my dad says when I sit on the sofa in his living room again.

"I don't have the kind of responsibilities Megan has," I say. I still can't stand the bitch, but I have to admit she's a busy woman.

"Her husband's a deadbeat," my dad insists.

I haven't been around Megan and her family much. When my dad got out of the hospital they had us over for dinner, but it was awkward. Kyle appears to be a long-suffering house husband who takes care of everything domestic, while she brings home the bacon. Their kids, Leah and Aaron, are smart and very polite, but they seemed scared of me. It's hard to get a real understanding of a family in a short visit, though, and of course I know impressions can be deceiving.

"You've never believed anyone was good enough for your daughters," I remind him. He rolls his eyes and grunts.

The doorbell rings. I get up to answer it.

"Hey," I say, opening the door, surprised to see Smith Walker.

"Hey yourself. Are you okay?"

His green eyes are so kind. I'd been tough through Armand's interview, but seeing the look on Smith's face reminds me how bad it really was.

"You mean the interview?" I try to scoff but if comes out very indelicately, more like a snort.

"I watched from my mom's condo. I'd noticed your car here earlier, and when I saw how the interview went… Well, I raced right over, such as it is." He smiles and reaches for my hand. I give it to him.

I shrug. I don't feel the pressure to be brave in front of Smith that I felt with my dad.

"Who's here?" my dad calls out.

"Smith Walker," I reply.

"Bring him in here."

I've gleaned that Smith has made quite a success of himself: he lives in our old neighborhood only one street from Megan, he has his mom set up here, and he owns a company that appears to be thriving despite the terrible economy. I bet my dad still thinks of him as the upstart from the poor side of town, though.

Smith nods and pastes on a formal smile as he makes his way down the hall toward the living room. "Hello, Mr. Golden."

"Did you see that gay bastard on television, making my D-Lynn look like a fool?"

"I saw the interview," Smith replies.

"Well, she's still a Golden in this town. And that means something." My dad juts out his chin as if he expects Smith to disagree or challenge him.

Smith nods patiently until my dad reaches for the remote and turns on the television.

I walk up the hall toward the kitchen and Smith follows. "How about I buy you a drink?" he whispers.

"I don't think I want to go out tonight," I say. I'm more scared than ever to be seen in public. On the other hand, I fear going back to my hotel room to find the walls have been painted lavender.

"I know a really quiet place," Smith says.

I try not to notice how difficult it is for Smith to climb into the driver's seat of his Ford. He puts his cane carefully beside me, with the curved handle looped over the console. I rest my knee against the straight part. It's a beautiful and sturdy cane, made of oak in a warm hue, with a leather grip on the handle. It's as impeccable as Smith's car, his jacket, his gloves; he obviously takes great care of everything. I look down at my worn out cowboy boots that have salt stains on the toes and hope he doesn't see me as a complete mess, like Armand does.

"Lucky you, you get my good side," he says.

When he faces the windshield, I can only see his right profile, and he's the Smith Walker I have always known. A bit older of course, but the years look good on him.

"Promise we're going somewhere quiet?"

"Trust me," he says.

He turns so that I see both the familiar side of him and where he's been changed. I do trust him, and that's no small wonder tonight.

"Oops, I forgot I was giving you my good side." Smith turns to face the windshield and starts the car.

I'm so stung by all the things Armand said, they come back to me in little waves of hurt. I sniffle and Smith reaches over and pats my arm.

"Don't let him get you down, Gwen. He was being a jerk."

"Maybe he was finally telling the truth," I say, my voice

cracking a little. "Armand always told me he loved my paintings, but maybe he lied so I wouldn't know how bad I was, because being a good artist means so much to me. He probably thought it was kinder to let me see myself as a talented painter instead of being as hopeless at that as I am at everything else."

Smith turns to look at me again with his warm green eyes that are unchanged from the first time I saw him, when we were both kids. I wouldn't recognize myself from back then, but I would know him anywhere.

"Do you want to know what I see when I look at you?" he asks.

I bite my lip. I'm not sure if I can take any more honest feedback tonight—my heart might break right in two. Smith touches my cheek.

"When I look at you Gwen, I see a girl who was never afraid to stick up for someone that needed help. I see a woman who makes everyone around her feel at ease. I see a brilliant painter. I don't see a fallen celebrity because you were always a real person to me, Gwen. Not an idea, not an image. When I look at you, I see the real you."

I put my hand over his on my cheek. If I could find my voice without blubbering, I would thank Smith. I would tell him that the reverse is also true. I would tell him that he hasn't changed a bit.

chapter twelve

caroline

Suzie blows a swath of hair out of her eyes that had escaped her ponytail. There are also several strands clinging to the back of her sweaty neck, and some plastered to the side of her face. My sister is a redhead, and her skin matches her hair when she works hard.

She adjusts her jeans over her stomach unselfconsciously. While I might go up and down ten pounds over the course of a year, Suzie stays plump. I used to feel somewhat superior that I could at least enjoy thin times, but lately I wonder if steadiness isn't a smarter course.

I pause to wipe my forehead. I'm cleaning a paint roller in the sink while Suzie scrubs mildew from the tub in an upstairs bathroom of my new house.

"How will I ever repay you?" I ask.

"Honestly, I don't think it's possible. This is so *gross*."

I chortle a little in exhaustion. "I'm so glad I didn't let the kids see this place when I first got the keys. They'd be plagued by nightmares."

"Thanks a lot! Now I'll probably see this tub in my dreams," she says.

I'm so glad Suzie is here. I had insisted I could tackle this house alone, but she said like hell I could. She started working alongside me, and now I realize how much I needed her.

"The primer is dry, so I'll start rolling the color on. Sunny Day should make us forget how nasty this room was," I say.

I shudder a little, despite my words. I still get the heebie-jeebies when I think of how horribly neglected this house had been. I'm proud, too, because I feel like we're healing it, one layer of filth cleared away, one repair at a time.

I look at my watch and calculate. "I should be able to get two coats on before I have to go meet the bus. How's that looking?"

"Vile. But underneath the cooties it looks good. I don't think there's any permanent damage."

"Thank goodness."

Suzie looks as spent as I feel. Over the past two weeks she has helped me shovel out this house on the far end of our neighborhood. The family who owned it had left their creditors in a hurry, and it was in absolutely obscene condition, beginning with the fish tank full of decaying creatures and stench, progressing to piles of garbage that seemed more suited to a third world city than a Midwestern suburb—and I haven't even seen what's under the lumps of snow in the back yard. This house was as "as is" as possible. The dumpster I hired has already been emptied three times.

Every weekday since I've had access, when I haven't been working at the library I've been working here. I traded all my shifts this week so that I could be here nonstop, from the moment I put the kids on the bus until forty minutes before they get dropped off. That leaves me just enough time to race home, shower, dress, and get outside to meet the bus.

June, Joy and James haven't seen this house yet because I want to wait until it's clean, and pretty, and homey. I can't bear to imagine June's face if she'd seen it when I first walked in. I had a good cry then, and I've had at least one daily since. But with the place emptied, the floors sanded and refinished, and most surfaces scrubbed and painted fresh, the tears don't come as frequently now.

Most nights I fall asleep ten minutes after putting the kids to bed: deep, dreamless sleeps that make me wake in shocked outrage when the alarm goes off in the morning. I believe it must be wrong, that surely I just shut my eyes a minute ago, and there's *no possible way* morning could have already arrived. James gave me a name for it, coined a year ago when he had a night that went by too fast. He called it a "blink night."

"Did you get a hold of Blake?" Suzie asks, bent over a corner of the tub.

My face stings red. "The realtor I mentioned talked to him. He signed the papers."

"He's lucky you were able to find a buyer. Some husband and father! Leaving you without any consideration as to how you were going to make payments!"

"Actually Suzie," I say, dreading every word because I should have said them months ago. "He didn't know we were in trouble with the house. He's sent money for the kids' activities and expenses, but I wanted to make the mortgage payments myself."

Suzie sits up and turns to look at me. "What?"

"You remember when he first left, I started working full time but I felt like I was losing touch with the kids. For a few weeks running they saw you more than they saw me."

She wipes her forehead on the back of her hand without taking her eyes from mine. "And?"

"And I never told Blake when I cut back my hours. I was too proud to tell him I couldn't pay for the house—I wanted to prove I could make it on my own."

"But you couldn't." She shakes her head and turns back to her task. For a while we work in silence.

"What did he say when he found out?"

"I don't know. The realtor spoke with him."

"Oh."

Within that single word I hear a thousand unspoken questions and judgments.

"I never claimed to know how to do any of this, Suzie. I'm sure I've made mistakes at every turn; I know I have. But I'r. doing the best I know how to do!"

She heaves a big sigh and I wonder if she's thinking back to our mom, who just couldn't seem to make a good decision to save her life. I realize now that it wasn't like she was staring down a lot of decent options and set out to always pick the worst one. Maybe she did the best she could, too. At least I know I'm doing some things right: my kids are safe and healthy.

They know they're loved.

"I see that you're doing your best, Caroline. And you know what? Despite being too proud, you're doing pretty great."

"You're so full of crap! I'm not only a stinking mess, I'm dragging you down with me." I look up from the sink to Suzie's disgusting progress and laugh. And she laughs with me.

Though I'm achy from work, over-caffeinated, and bleary from too many blink nights in a row, I've asked Gwendolyn Golden to come over this evening.

It seems bizarre to think that I used to idolize her. Now I truly feel sorry for her. Gwendolyn's supposed friend blasted her on television, and she has gone from living in a mansion to living in a hotel room. When I asked what day she'd scheduled her moving van to come so I could make sure my stuff was out in time, she fell apart.

Gwendolyn confided that she doesn't own anything. I asked where she planned to sit, and sleep, and she actually started to cry! She said she has to furnish the house from scratch on a small budget. It doesn't help matters that since Armand's interview she can't walk into a store without drawing a crowd. She said she wouldn't be able to decide on anything anyway.

I offered to help her order some basics online.

She's due here any minute. I have the kids tucked into bed, and a plate of leftovers warming for Gwendolyn. She looks too thin, especially when I stand next to her and notice that her legs are not only a foot longer than mine, but substantially narrower. I try never to stand next to her.

When Gwendolyn arrives, we get down to business right away. She eats while I go over the list of basics I think she'll need. She doesn't have anything to add to or delete from it. I begin to show her some things online, but in every case she defers to my opinion. So I basically choose what I like, working my way down the list.

She asks if she can borrow some paper from a drawing tablet on the kids' art shelf, and soon she's happily doodling while I spend her money outfitting this house, which will soon be hers. I would be uncomfortable making all the selections if I didn't already know what she likes: she likes Armand's style, which is virtually identical to mine, except mine is cheaper.

I'm disgusted that he didn't help her when he came to visit. I remember she'd been so excited when she asked if she could show him through the house. She clearly expected Armand's advice to guide her, but I don't think he did anything at all.

"I saw the interview your old partner did," I tell her when I take a break from the computer to get a glass of water. I notice she ate her whole plate of leftovers.

Gwendolyn frowns over her pencil.

I step closer to see what she's drawing. "That's amazing!" I say, my heart warming at the beautiful sketch she is making from a photograph of my kids. Somehow the pencil captures more detail in their faces than the photo, and I don't know how that's possible, but it's true.

Gwendolyn shrugs her shoulders and sighs. I think back to Armand saying in his interview that she was a fluffy house wares painter and nothing more.

"That is really beautiful," I tell her.

Gwendolyn looks up at me with an expression that brings to mind the time that Joy came home with a sad face on one of her papers. She was so hurt, so ashamed, so unsure of herself. A substitute teacher had apparently not known it was an advanced math sheet of problems the kids hadn't learned yet. Joy had taken it from the extra work file because she had finished her assignment early. When she proudly showed it to the sub, he went through and corrected it in red marker and put the sad face on.

Joy was crushed when she showed that paper to me. She cried like I have rarely heard her. It took so much convincing that evening for her to believe that she really is smart, with the evidence of a goddamn red sad face working against her. I don't think she had ever doubted herself like that before.

"My favorite things have your designs on them," I tell Gwendolyn, pointing out a hand-painted side table I'd gotten as a birthday present a year ago, the tablecloth's design, throw pillows on the window seat. "I love all these, but I had no idea you could do something like this, too. You're really talented," I tell her, admiring the drawing.

She nods a little, looking back down at her page, and I see a teardrop hit the paper.

"Armand is a complete idiot," I say. "I felt bad when that interviewer turned the tables on him, but now I wish he'd done worse."

"Stuart turned the tables?" Gwen asks, looking worried.

"You didn't watch?"

"I saw only part of it."

I can't imagine walking away from a television interview about me! I'd not only be watching, but taking notes and keeping score.

"He tried to corner Armand into admitting he was gay, once and for all, for the live viewing audience."

"I didn't know that happened," Gwendolyn says, shaking her head.

I find it surreal that she is hearing what every tabloid consumer already knows about her friend's life from me.

"What did Armand say?" she asks.

"That's when he finally chose to keep his mouth shut, the self-serving ass."

"He's not, though. He's a good person," she says.

I can't imagine being so forgiving. "They showed clips of interviews with men Armand had dated over the years. All of them were formerly in the closet, too, because apparently he only dated guys as scared to come out as he was."

"Yeah," Gwendolyn says, nodding sadly.

"I mean, why can't he just come out and say, 'I'm gay. So what?'"

"I know he would if he could, but it's complicated," she says.

Her eyes are huge and she looks so thin that I start fixing her another plate of leftovers without asking first.

"Nothing is complicated. You do what you're supposed to

do, and if you screw up you deal with the consequences. It's simple," I say. As if I live by that credo myself.

All told, it takes three hours to order the essentials Gwendolyn will need—for her that's not a tremendous amount of stuff: a bed, pillows, linens, kitchen tools, a dinette set, a sofa, coffee table, lamps, and rugs. That stretches her budget to the absolute limit. I do a lot of comparison shopping, and find free shipping deals, and scan a thousand reviews in the process. The house will still be woefully empty, but she'll at least have the most basic basics once everything arrives.

She paid so little attention to the choices, other than saying she didn't want anything lavender, that I could have set her up with anything. Gwendolyn has grown on me in our few visits, though. It feels good to help her, especially since I've received so much help from Suzie. I am exhausted by the time Gwendolyn gets up to leave. She hands me the lovely drawing it took her all this time to finish.

"It's gorgeous," I say.

I wish she believed me. I think it's amazing that someone I thought had all the confidence in the world a few weeks ago turns out to be as full of misgivings as I am.

"Wait a minute," I tell her. I quickly gather up a little basket of goodies, including some fruit, snacks I pack in the kids' lunches, and a Tupperware container full of more leftovers. I tuck in some tea. She's already driving away when I realize that we didn't order her a shower curtain, towels, or a bath mat!

The phone rings and I look at the handset on the counter to see that it's Blake again. I have been avoiding his calls, and the argument I'm sure we'll have, which I realize I deserve for getting in so deep without asking for help. I look at the clock and am irritated he'd call at eleven p.m., knowing the kids are asleep. That concern probably didn't occur to an independent bachelor with all the space in the world around him, though. Prick.

"Trying to wake the kids?"

"Carrie? I can't believe you actually answered!"

"I'm a surprise a minute," I say. As good as I felt a few moments ago, helping Gwendolyn and feeling like I had my shit together at least in comparison to her, I regress quickly talking to Blake.

"I wish you had told me about the house. It was embarrassing to hear it from a stranger."

"I wish you had told me about Francine Robinson. It was embarrassing to hear it from Claire Wiltz in the grocery store."

He takes a deep breath and lets it out. I almost hang up. I don't want to even hear him breathe.

"I've told you a thousand times that Francine is a colleague of mine, not a love interest. You know that Claire Wiltz is the worst gossip in town, and she never cares if what she says is true."

"What kind of husband and father of three claims to need space if he's not having an affair?" I demand.

"Me."

"Luckily you're thousands of miles away, then. Bastard."

"I'm coming home."

"You have no home here!" I hang up on him. The phone rings again ten seconds later.

"I'm moving back to Riveredge. I'm done with this project and I'm going to work at headquarters."

I realize that I never imagined Blake in the new house. I felt like I would be leaving him behind, along with my pain and anger, when I move three streets lower into the subdivision.

"You can't live with us."

"I'll get an apartment then," he says. "I'm sorry I needed some time to think, Carrie. I realize I was selfish. I love you and the kids, and I want to try and make it up to you."

It's pathetic how much his saying the words *I'm sorry* means to me. I think they're more powerful the less adequate to the damages they are, because they carry such pathos in them, such failure.

"I'll be moving back in two weeks. Can I call the kids tomorrow when they get home from school and tell them the news?"

"Not unless you're damn sure you're coming."

"I'm positive."

"Positive, huh? Like you'd swear to it, like you'd make a vow?"

"I know I've got a lot to make up for. I don't blame you for being angry and doubting me. I'll call the kids tomorrow. I love you, Carrie."

I hang up the phone because I'll be damned if I'll let him hear me cry anymore.

chapter thirteen

armand

I'm a hit!

For a minute there I worried that the skeletons Trey dragged out of my closet had made me look like a confused floozy. So what if that's exactly what I've been? I still don't want everyone else to know! Nobody, not even the most fame-seeking rising star, not even teenage Madonna when she already wanted to rule the world but was still stuck in Bay City, Michigan, wants to tell *every* little thing. I don't even like disclosing the secret ingredient which makes my soups simmer, let alone who I did what with, when, or how.

I needn't have worried. Trey called me up the day after the interview like we were best buddies. He said the focus groups loved me, and *So Perfect* had already gotten tons of "sympathetic" emails and phone calls about me. Maybe I should have been offended by that word choice, like I'm Tiny Tim, or Oliver Twist, or some other Dickensian sad sack. I'm not above wanting a little sympathy, though. Lord, no! I was relieved. I confess that I *loved* that spotlight shining down on me.

On interview day, I'd had the time of my life getting my hair and make-up done in the star seat. I chose my clothes with the help of the cutest wardrobe guy on God's green earth. I was the center of attention for once! When the cameras lit up, I did, too. I thought I could just stay right there on that elevated sofa looking out at my dining room audience for*ever*. I'd have died happy if lightening had struck—I'm always on the lookout anyway.

It hadn't been *all* fun and games. There were moments when I could almost feel my mother's judging eyes on me, watching from her ass-imprinted throne in Praiseville. When I was forced to traipse down memory lane, seeing clips of old lovers who said I should just come on out into the open, I kept thinking: *Oh Gerald with your handsome smile, oh Mike always saying the right thing, oh Norman you bald hottie on the lookout for your next fifteen minutes of fame, and my dear Sam who I loved with all my heart for four solid weeks until your wife found out, I hope none of you ever run into my mama in a dark alley. Because there ain't a single one of you that she couldn't wallop but good, honey.*

I had been afraid that the reviews would be bad, that no one would like me, and that I'd never ever *never* get to have my hair and makeup done for cameras and fans again. I still prayed I wouldn't have to give it up. The applause from that live audience…Oh! I got teary-eyed when I saw my old suburban Jen there, and touched that she'd brought along all the other Jens. She slipped me a photograph of their stylist Carl, and let's just say I think I might be *way* overdue for some highlights.

When everyone had gone and I walked through my Grand Dame of a house, I thought that might have been the best day I'd ever have. My big fear was that I'd wake up the next morning to find out the world decided I was terrible again.

But I'm a hit!

Along with Trey telling me that I am a hot commodity (something I'd always suspected despite his uptight corporate lip service), he said I could access some of my frozen stock options. I didn't waste precious time that he could use to change his mind; I cashed out some stock dough and went off to St. Thomas.

To tell you the truth, I was in hiding. Trey has always sat on one of my shoulders and whispered in my ear like a little devil, but with Gwendolyn gone I had no angel on the other side to balance him out. More interview offers poured in after the one I did with Stuart, and Trey was acting like he was my handler, telling me what I should or shouldn't do, and how I should or shouldn't do it.

I don't trust Trey to hold a ladder while I change a light bulb, let alone keep my career interests in mind if they don't happen to align with his. So, right before I left for St. Thomas, I hired an agent. Josie reps some of my favorite decorating and cooking stars, and she promised to help me get a bigger piece of my own action. Josie's first tasks as my advocate: tell Trey about her new role, and examine my *So Perfect* contract.

I tanned and lounged, but I grew bored on the beach. I came home early.

I haven't been able to get Gwendolyn off my mind. She was on the cover of a tabloid I picked up for the flight home. I haven't spoken to her since the interview aired, so I figure it's time to dial her up.

I stall. I guess I've been stalling about making the call all week. I haven't watched the interview myself, and to tell you the truth my memory of it is kind of a blur. That interview was as fun and fast as a four-story waterslide, but I don't remember every little twist and turn, just that I made a big splash. I decide it's probably a good idea to remember exactly what I said before I talk to Gwendolyn.

If this posh hotel suite had a proper kitchen, I'd make a batch of caramel corn. Cuing up the interview makes me think back to cozy times when Gwendolyn and I sat on the sofa and watched *House Hunters*. That show is fabulous! When you see a couple in their home, taking care of their cats and dogs, making dinner, and just living, it doesn't matter if they're gay or straight. They're just people, same as anyone else. I love that show.

I appear on the screen, waving and smiling. I couldn't have been more nerved up, not even if my mother had been sitting in the front row, so it's a nice surprise to see that I look cool and easy. I'm very relieved that I picked the right sweater. My jeans look good. I'm glad I wore those shoes.

So far, so good. I like me!

My smile gets a little smaller, and a little smaller, as the interview goes on though. It gets wiped right off my mouth when I think of Gwendolyn watching, with her slow loris eyes getting more giant and more slow loris-y by the second. Six days have gone by since the interview aired and I haven't even called her. And she said she trusted me.

I can see the interview was edited to make her look terrible. They kept anything I said that was mean and took away the sweet things I said about her, and of course I said lots, because the kid *is* sweet. I guess I'd never thought about how much impact editing could have, since I'd only seen it used to tighten up DIY segments. I didn't know it could be so sinful.

As my stomach continues to sink, I realize that I can't blame it all on the editing. I still said what I said, and laughed when I laughed. I cover my eyes through parts of it. When it's all over, I turn it off and hang my head.

In retrospect, I know I acted terrible. But retrospect has never been a friend to me. It's the bruised and banged up look Lenny Nelson gave me in math class the day after meeting with my mama's broom handle. It's the credit card bill in college I had no way of paying, jacked up sky high by the night I got drunk and bought the house three rounds. It's the realization that I treated Gwendolyn so badly six nights ago, whether I knew it then or not.

I gather up the courage to call her. I fear she'll shout at me. She'll say I'm an opportunist, like Norman did back in that NYC hotel room a month ago.

"Hi, Armand."

Gwendolyn sounds like some of the air has been let out of her and she's sort of thudding along like a half-flat bike tire, or a playground ball that renders a decent game of Four Square all but impossible.

"I'm so sorry about the interview! I hadn't watched it back until now. Just yell at me and get it over with," I say.

She doesn't reply.

"Come on now! Please tell me off. I deserve it."

"Tell yourself off, if it makes you feel better. I don't have much to say." She sighs and I imagine her deflating even more.

"Please yell at me. I'm so sorry."

She is quiet for a minute and I'm scared she'll hang up. I feel like the pathetic girl in that demented *After School Special* I saw when I was a kid. The one who tries to impress her classmates, but she ends up scaring her pet bird to death instead. I think I was too young to follow the plot; all I remember is guilt, guilt, guilt.

"Do you hate me?" I ask in a panic.

"No."

"Then talk to me. Tell me three things and I'll be satisfied."

"What things?"

"Any things."

"Fine. One: heather blue is definitely your on-camera color."

Oh sweet relief; she's still with me. "I agree with you there. Now tell me some bad ones. Two?"

"You're a natural when you're allowed to ham it up for a live audience."

She's so right! "You're down to your last one so don't give me another compliment. Be ruthless! I'm going to brace myself and take it like a man."

"I still love you," she says.

"Really?"

"Yup."

"Oh thank God! I'm so glad to hear you haven't written me off. I'm going to send you out some baked goods and hair treatments right away."

"No, thanks."

"But you sound thin, and your hair sounds witchy."

"With the nice things I said to you, that's what you choose to say to me?"

"You're right. I'm sorry. Are you all moved in yet?" I picture the cute house she fell in love with all emptied out and it gives me a tummy ache.

"One more week."

"I want to buy you a present. How about living room furniture? Do you still have the measurements?"

"Caroline helped me order some stuff online."

"Caroline? My little savant?" I remember her wearing gloves and a surgical mask and saying she was going to put her rancid new place together in three weeks. I knew it wasn't possible, the poor thing.

"The woman I bought the house from, yeah."

"What stuff did she help you order?"

"Things I could afford. I'll have dishes, a bed, a couch, and a lot more. She had it all on a list," Gwendolyn says in that far-off way that makes me suspect she's got a paintbrush in her hand at this very moment and is only half listening to me.

"That was sweet of her," I say loudly, just to be sure I'm heard.

"She's very nice, and resourceful."

"Is she? I hired an agent who's fielding some offers. Do you think Caroline would want to be my assistant?"

"I doubt it, but I can give her your number."

"Why do you doubt it?" I hear that I sound pouty, but I don't blame myself.

"She doesn't really like you."

"Why not?"

"I don't think she liked your interview."

"Well let's forget her for the moment then. Tell me about you and Walter."

"There's nothing to tell."

"Then tell me about the horror movie guy."

"What guy?"

"At the airport I saw a picture of you with a guy they called Scar Face."

"Scar Face?" She sounds so sad that I'm sure her eyes cover up her whole head.

"Who is he?"

"Oh God… He's a wonderful man, way too good to be dragged into my public stoning. I used to date him. He's been in an accident since then."

I saw the guy's picture, so I know it must have been a really rough accident to take him from being cute enough to date Gwendolyn to how he looks now. I mean *wow*. I've seen her hometown, though, and let's just say it's pretty small. I guess I wouldn't be surprised if she has also dated her second cousin and her history teacher at some point in time.

"You used to date him? Why'd you break up?" I ask.

"My parents didn't approve." She sounds utterly flattened.

"How are you spending your time?" I realize that's a dumb question as soon as it's out of my mouth. There's only one thing Gwendolyn likes to do in her free time. I correct myself before she gets a chance to answer: "What have you been painting?"

"I don't want to talk about that with you."

I can almost see her looking up at me, with her scary hair, and her cheekbones too prominent because the poor kid doesn't know how to feed herself properly.

"I'm sorry I made that stupid comment in the interview, but I had just noticed the paint on the sofa. I didn't mean it. I even said so right afterward, but they cut it out. You're brilliant! The entire Met should be covered with your stuff."

"You suck," she whispers.

"Come on, I didn't mean it."

"Well, just remember that paybacks are hell."

"What does that mean?" I ask.

"Maybe I'll say something mean about you during my interview."

"You don't have it in you to be mean. Wait. What interview are you talking about?"

"Trey said if I do an interview, he'll free up my stock options. He said if I don't, he'll sue me for breach of contract. I haven't decided yet, but I'll probably end up saying yes, as long as he releases me from the contract. I want all this behind me."

"Okay," I say, trying not to panic on Gwendolyn's behalf, but also feeling like panic is definitely in order. "When are you taping?"

"In a week, if I agree. Stuart Bolder would come here to do it."

I noticed during my interview that Stuart's dimples looked huge; I wondered if his makeup girl did something to make them stand out. His tie appeared to have been custom made to highlight his eyes. He's been acting like this scandal's the best thing that has ever happened to him. Now he's the go-to guy for updates on the story for several national entertainment shows, and he and Trey are suddenly two peas in a pod.

Though the idea of Gwendolyn being raked over the coals makes me scared and angry, I can't help fearing what this could mean for me. Is it possible the tide of public opinion will turn and wash me out into the sea of has-beens, like a forgotten flip flop or a plastic shovel? They edited my answers to make Gwendolyn look her worst; will they have her throw cold water right back on me?

No, I'm safe there. Gwendolyn doesn't have an ounce of meanness in her. And that wouldn't fit Trey's spin on this—he's been courting me so hard I'm worried he's gonna propose soon. He's been working diligently to make Gwendolyn into a laughing stock, trying to deflect attention from *So Perfect's* deception by acting like it was all her fault and hers alone. No, I'm not in trouble, but they'll be out to make the poor kid look as bad as possible.

"We've got to get you all prettied up!" I say fiercely.

"I couldn't care less what I look like. I just want this over. I never want to be on television, or in a newspaper or tabloid, ever again."

"Do you have any skeletons in your closet there?" I ask.

"No. Why?"

"That reporter from Stuart's station is tenacious. I don't know how she managed to dig up my old beaus and get them on camera, but if you've got any secrets, she'll find them."

Gwendolyn sighs. "You were my only secret."

"Hi there, Armand!" my new agent, Josie, says when I dial her up. "Are you tanned and ready to get your career in gear?"

I love my agent. She's my own personal cheerleader.

"Yup, tanned and ready. Hey, I hear Gwendolyn Golden is doing an interview next week without me."

"Oh? Well that should mean some good opportunities for you. I'll see what I can find out. I want to talk to you about the interesting proposals I've been fielding, too, so let's get together soon."

"Okay. Are you sure people still like me?"

"Of course! They love you, Armand."

From personal cheerleader to righteous heckler… As I dial her number, I picture my mama sitting in her Praiseville shoebox.

"Son? Is that you?"

"Hello, ma'am. I'm just returning your calls."

"Armand, I read in one of those filthy tabloids that you're in St. Thomas."

Not too filthy to read, I guess. I don't say it though, I just think it.

"I'm back again, ma'am."

"Oh. Well. I've never been to St. Thomas, you know."

"Did you want to go?" I ask, sort of high and strained.

"You didn't ask me, did you? So I guess it doesn't matter if I would've wanted to go or not."

I imagine my mama in her white orthopedic shoes and one of her flower-printed tent dresses beside me in St. Thomas. I don't think there's a bathing suit in the whole world that could hold her.

"It didn't cross my mind," I say.

"I suppose being famous makes you too busy for me?"

"Would you want to go on vacation with me sometime? I mean, would your church friends approve of that?" I ask, my curiosity overcoming my fear of a lecture full of insults.

"I guess I could go sometime," she says, like she'd be doing me a big favor. "You would have to wear clothes and not run around half naked, though. Gladdy Prinster said she did a Google search and saw pictures of you in St. Thomas wearing less than Jesus on the cross. I suppose it wouldn't hurt to go around with you next time to make sure you behave yourself."

"That sounds like a lot of fun, ma'am," I say, hiding my sarcasm the best I can.

"Of course it would be better for you and your wife Gwendolyn to patch things up and take a trip together first. I don't approve of her extramarital romancing at all, Armand. I wrote to your wife about it, you know."

"You wrote to Gwendolyn?"

"Yes. Gladdy Prinster found me her address on the world wide web."

"And what did you say to her?" I ask.

"That you two need to come to Jesus and fix your rift. That marriage is blessed by God, and as such, it's meant to last forever. But you know that already, Armand. I know you already know that."

As I unpack my suitcase, I try to banish several things from my brain: hurting Gwendolyn's feelings with the stupid crack about her painting skills, worrying that Trey is mad I hired Josie, and wondering if my mother will ever accept reality. If I could only delete one image from my mind, though, I know which one I'd pick: Gladdy Prinster Googling me.

chapter fourteen

smith

"It's not like 'Scar Face' can chase her down and hit her on the head like a caveman," my brother Jones sagely says. "He'd be too slow to catch her, and he'd need both hands to drag her back to the cave."

Overly generous guffawing by my obnoxious family brings happy tears of mirth to many eyes. Mine included, and I'm only slightly ashamed to admit it. So what if our humor isn't the most refined in the world? It's all in good fun, doled out equally, and has its basis in love. That has always been enough for me. Within our family, joking about hardship has always been a shared coping mechanism.

"Are you sure you want to marry into this nonsense?" I ask Carmen, the bride-to-be, who's sporting her jazzy new diamond. I recently consented to be Taylor's best man, and tonight's dinner is in honor of their engagement.

"I can't wait!" she says, beaming.

"Just ask her on a date, Uncle Smith!" my four-year-old nephew says.

"That would be way too easy," his father, my brother Siler, butts in. "Uncle Smith likes to take his time in matters of love. He's on the hundred year plan with Ms. Golden."

My family teasing me about Gwen makes me feel like I'm in high school again. As I did then, I try to keep my feelings to myself. In a large and close-knit family, though, there's no surer way to make it loud dinner table conversation.

We're dining at Siler's tonight. His wife Janet seems to

have the highest tolerance for Walkers, so she often hosts the "extra" dinners. Unfortunately Siler and Janet have kept up the confounding convention of using last names as first names that my parents began. Their children are Miller, Gibbs, and Crane. I wish I was kidding, or that they had at least spared their daughter.

"Pwease pass the buttah, Unca Scow Face," Crane sweetly lisps from my left. Jones snickers beside her and I know he put her up to it. I try to scare her by growling viciously but she just giggles. I pass the butter.

My family has been using my tabloid nickname tonight, apparently in a concerted effort to take away the power of the insult. I think overall the approach works well. When you hear people say them with love, otherwise harsh words begin to take on a new tone, until maybe they don't sting quite so much. My mom and Taylor haven't addressed me as Scar Face; apparently they're more squeamish than three-year-old Crane.

The dinner table banter thankfully shifts from my prospects with Gwen, to my mom's senior community romance. Though my dad has been dead for ten years, my mother's new boyfriend Caleb seems to be a constant source of wonder and befuddlement to the entire clan. She blushes when Siler teases her about him.

Janet encouraged me to invite Gwen tonight, but there were several reasons why I didn't. First, whenever I observe the table manners of my assembled kin, which I try to avoid doing as much as possible to preserve my appetite, I simply can't imagine bringing her to a family dinner. Second, today was her moving day.

I sent my handyman Steve over there this morning with the things sent from the Scenic house that I have been storing for Gwen. Steve told me about the circuslike atmosphere he found, so I went myself with lunch around noon. That brings up the biggest reason why I didn't ask Gwen to come here for dinner tonight—she has important plans. She's taping an interview with the reporter who helped Armand Leopold skewer her two weeks ago.

Gwen told me about the interview only after she'd already

agreed to do it. She said she doesn't have a choice in the matter. I wanted to talk her out of it, but I didn't want to overstep my bounds.

The plan had been to tape the interview at the local television station. But today Gwen told me that now it's going to be at her new house. Shelly Simon got the idea when she went there this morning to ask Gwen some preliminary questions.

I didn't like the sound of it. I didn't like the look of it either. Gwen's house is empty, and I heard Ms. Simon say "riches to rags" to a cameraman.

I've been worried about Gwen since Armand's interview aired. Her nerves have grown taut and fragile from the unfavorable attention. She can't wholly avoid hearing what people say by living a hermit's life, especially when her dad and sister keep telling her the worst of it. Gwen seems to think that tonight will bring an end to all the attention, but somehow I doubt that taping a national interview is the wisest step if your goal is to disappear.

I might've stayed around longer to see if there was any way to cancel the damn thing, but Walter Owens from the hotel showed up with a housewarming basket the size of Rhode Island. He told Gwen what a wonderful time he'd had the night before, and I suddenly wanted to get the hell out of there. I told her to call me if she needed anything.

After what happened the night of Armand's interview, though, I won't blame Gwen if she never calls me again.

I had wanted to comfort her, and since she wasn't up to going out in public, I brought her home with me. I hadn't stopped to worry or second guess myself. I drove us away from Gordy Golden's condo feeling like I was rescuing her, from a father who was embarrassed not only for her but by her, from strangers who readily believed the negative things they had heard, from old acquaintances who might be glad to see the local celebrity brought down a few notches.

I felt like I was protecting Gwen; I felt strong. When I pulled into my driveway, I could tell she was impressed by my home. My garage has been adapted to make my life easy, so I got out of the car as smoothly as possible.

My housecleaner had been in earlier. Though I live in very little of the large house, and I spend most of my days working, Michelle comes in twice a week. She used to come every other week, and that was perfect. Then her husband Bryan was laid off from his construction job and Michelle asked if he could wash the windows and re-stain the decks, anything at all. I already struggle to keep my handyman Steve, a father of two, busy between my company's commercial properties and my house. I couldn't very well hire out the same work twice, even if Taylor does call me "the Rising Tide," because he says I'm determined to raise all the boats around me. Whenever he calls me that, I remind him that he of all people shouldn't complain.

"What can I get you?" I asked from the bar in the sunken living room after I'd settled Gwen on the built-in sofa. I switched on the lights in the back yard so that the wall of windows gave us something pretty to look at. Give her something, I should say, because I simply watched Gwen.

"What are you having?"

"How about wine?" I checked my watch to make sure it was okay. If I have a drink too close to when I need my pain pill I get an upset stomach. I had slipped on the ice a few days before, and I needed every dose allowable by law in order to keep cheerful and keep moving.

"Sounds wonderful."

I opened a bottle and poured two glasses. I made my way around the bar and brought her glass to her before making a round trip to retrieve mine. She let me do this, and I found it refreshing, and respectful, too, if that doesn't sound strange. Many people rush to help me, like they'd grab a child's hand away from a hot stove, or thrust a napkin on an elderly relative who has become a messy eater. It felt good to be treated like a regular man.

She looked around with wide, interested eyes. "I've always wanted to see inside this house. The Fosters never put it on the architectural tour. I think they were shy."

I smile. This house had been in the Foster family since it

was built in 1929. The Fosters were reclusive and private to a degree some would call insane. I like that Gwen simply thought of them as "shy." When Sophie Foster died five years ago and the house went on the market, people flocked here as if Geraldo were opening Al Capone's vault. It turned out to be just an ordinary house, in pristine original condition. Homes in this small and exclusive neighborhood rarely become available. Within the small world of Riveredge, an address here means you have arrived. I had jumped at the chance to buy it.

"Want to take a walk around? You can go anywhere you like."

"Yes, let's!"

I noticed that she had kicked off her cowboy boots. Barefoot, she carried her glass with her as she pointed out small architectural details I'd never really noticed. I set my glass on a table and followed after her.

Other women I had brought home in the past, the pre-accident past, had been impressed with the house. It's considered to be a local architectural treasure, designed as it was by a man Frank Lloyd Wright referred to as his "spiritual son." Gwen was impressed by the home as an artist herself, as well as a woman who'd grown up near enough to see its chimney from her bedroom window. It felt odd to be the one to invite her inside for the first time. I never guessed I'd be able to unlock a door that had been previously closed to Gwen Golden.

Unlike other women, though, Gwen clearly didn't attribute any of the charm of my house's architecture to me just because I currently owned the building. She appreciated the lines and the setting; I was beside the point. When I realized that, it made sense to me. Gwen sees things differently than I do, and that's part of why I find her so intriguing. It's part habit, part the way she sees the world.

It took me ten minutes to follow her across the sunken living room, through the kitchen, and past the library where she stopped outside the master suite. I pointed inside, indicating that she should enter first, but she just smiled and folded her arms.

"After all the effort I expended getting here, you don't want to go in?" I asked like I was disappointed. I was careful to give her my good side.

"And here I thought you were a gentleman," she said. I tried to read her eyes, but the lighting in the hall was dim. I had done more walking that day than usual, and after my recent fall I'd been in a lot of pain.

Certain events seem like they should be immune from real world considerations. Like an astronaut circling the earth, or me standing outside my bedroom bantering with Gwen Golden. Some moments are so important, so otherworldly, that normal human concerns shouldn't rightly apply. But if the astronaut has a stomach bug, that colors his experience. My leg throbbed and it affected my ability to read Gwen's eyes.

"It looks pretty," she said as she peeked past me into the master bedroom. I saw her face redden and wondered if it was the glass of wine she'd finished that colored her cheeks, and hoped it wasn't.

"Hold up a minute. I want to show you something," I told her. It took me a while, but eventually I returned.

"You're kidding," she said, when I was halfway to her and she saw what I held carefully. She crossed to me and took the sheet of thick drawing paper on which she'd sketched the two of us at Riveredge Park.

"You mean you kept this?"

"Of course I did."

"For ten years? And then you were able to find it that quickly?"

"I keep it in a drawer, close at hand."

"If you like it so well, why do you keep it in a drawer?" she asked.

"I suppose I've been selfish."

She stayed at my side as we made our way back to the bar at the far end of the living room. I paused on the way to put her picture in the center of the mantle.

I poured us each another glass of wine. Though I knew I shouldn't have one, I wanted to pretend I was just a regular guy in a regular body. I sat close to where she sat with her bare feet tucked under her. She smiled and toasted:

"To old friends."

I clinked her glass. "To old friends made new again."

That's the moment when Jessie, bless her dingbat brain, rang the doorbell. The long walk from where I was sharing a cozy moment with Gwen to the front door nearly did me in.

"I forgot to have you sign the contract on the Eastman Road building, and it needs to go out first thing in the morning. You won't be in until after your physical therapy session, right?"

"Do you know how to use a telephone, Jessie?" I felt weary suddenly, like standing was just too much. I felt a cold line of sweat forming at my hairline.

"You look terrible, Smith," Jessie said before she looked up to see Gwen.

"Oh my *God*! You're Gwendolyn Golden!"

Gwen nodded and tried to smile but didn't quite pull it off.

"I saw the interview on television tonight. Are you angry with your husband? He's really handsome, isn't he?"

Jessie was positively giddy and I wondered, not for the first time, if her mother had dropped her on her head when she was a baby, or if perhaps a high fever had baked off some critical brain cells along the way. If she were a true member of my family and not just a cousin-in-law, we certainly would have come up with many more theories over loud dinners, and it's probably very good for Jessie that she's not wholly one of ours.

I had to grip the console table to steady myself. Jessie seemed torn for a moment, between fawning over Gwen and helping me, before my damn leg buckled and I leaned against the table to keep standing.

"Do you need medication?"

It was such a sexy thing to bring up, when five minutes before I'd been attempting to stoke up and rekindle Gwen's and my old flame.

"For God's sake Jessie, I'm not an invalid!"

The word hung in the air.

Jessie got my folding wheelchair from the hall closet, opened it, and pushed me down into it before I could protest. I don't know if I would have argued much, though I hated the situation. She wheeled me to my room, avoiding the sunken living room and its steps, and asked where my pills were. I let her get them for me and took them.

"Is this a date?" Jessie whispered, motioning toward the door.

"Do I look like a guy who'll get a date, Jess?"

I instantly regretted asking. She teared up, and it wasn't because I'd hurt her feelings. If I hadn't felt nauseous I would have wanted to break something.

"You'd be a great catch for any woman, Smith Walker. You're a bully and a baby, but you're one of the best men I know."

I nodded slightly and motioned to the door to indicate she was dismissed.

"I didn't see a car. Should I drive her home?"

"Yes," I made myself say. "Thanks, Jessie."

There was a knock on my door a minute later. I was still sitting in the damn wheelchair I rarely use anymore, only when I have overexerted myself or I'm ill. If I could have, I would have stepped right out of it then.

"Come in."

Gwen smiled without sympathy in her eyes, just regret, and I wished I had the energy and confidence to tell her to come close enough to kiss me. I thought of an ill astronaut again, waiting all his life for one moment, only to have his body betray him.

"I knew I could get you to come in here if I played my cards right."

She smiled. "I'm sorry you're feeling low. Can I help you get into bed?"

I almost made another joke, but I didn't. Sometimes even humor can't help.

"I'll be fine once my pain medicine kicks in. I overdid it today. This rarely happens."

"Thanks for tonight. You made me feel so much better."

"Like a knight in shining armor," I said, patting a chrome wheel with contempt.

"Yes, exactly," she said.

* * *

Back out of my head and back to dinner with the family, I feel a rough nudge from Siler on my right. He offers me brownies. I take one and set the pan down beside me on the long table with bench seating for twenty.

"Say goodnight to Uncle Smith, and I'll get you set up with a DVD," Janet says to Miller, Gibbs, and Crane. Each races up and gives me a giant bear hug, as if I'm as robust as any uncle out there.

"I think yo willy handsome," Crane whispers in my ear. She runs after her brothers, and blows me a kiss from the bottom step. I blow one back.

I always wanted to have a big family of my own, and I hate the fact that it's unlikely I'll ever fill my house with a wife and kids. Two of my brothers are married but don't have children yet. Cooper's wife is pregnant and due in a few months, and I've been told that Jones and his wife are "trying." I doubt Taylor and Carmen will be too far behind once the wedding turns into a framed portrait on the wall. This is a family-oriented family.

Everyone else is finished eating and many hands are making light work of clearing the table, washing the counters and pans, sweeping the floor, and loading the dishwasher.

Siler leans over to me. "A woman came by the station to ask some questions," he says in a confidential tone. Siler is a policeman.

"About what?" I ask.

"About your accident," he says.

"Who was it?"

"Her name was Shelley something. It was about that interview Gwendolyn's doing. I think she was just turning over as much ground as she could, to see if there were any worms worth digging up. You and Gwendolyn are together a lot, so apparently she's checking you out."

"Did she learn anything?"

"Nothing to learn," Siler says. That's another attribute of this family—loyalty.

Taylor, always solicitous and protective of me, sometimes to the point where I'd like to smack him upside the head, has come over and eavesdropped. He looks far more worried than Siler, and I'm inclined to agree. Gwen doesn't know the whole truth about the accident, and I'll be damned if I'll let some brazen interviewer blindside her with it for ratings points or whatever nonsense drives those people.

"When's the interview?" Taylor asks.

I look at the apple-shaped clock on the kitchen wall. "They're supposed to begin taping it at six." That's five minutes away. I reach for my cane and begin to stand. "I think I'd better get over there."

"I'll bring the car around," Taylor says, already halfway to the door.

chapter fifteen

gwendolyn

I look at the people assembled in my living room, which doesn't feel even a tiny bit like mine yet. I can't help but wonder if I'm making the biggest mistake of my life. Admittedly, that would be pretty big. I feel so uneasy while I watch Stuart Bolder and Shelley Simon go over notes in the corner that I'm overcome with temptation to call the whole thing off.

"What if I change my mind?" I ask.

Stuart looks up; his face is already perfected, his tie is adjusted just right, and his teeth are glaringly white and unrelentingly perfect. His dimples show too much and I'm strongly reminded of my classmate Elton Jorgensen, who never forgave Smith for coming to Riveredge Academy and proving on a daily basis that he was cooler, smarter, and wiser than Elton.

"Don't be silly, Gwendolyn. We're here to help you redeem yourself," Stuart says, as if he's already addressing multitudes.

"Listen to reason, Gwendolyn," Trey says calmly, like he's been on my side since day one, like we're in this together. "After the interview you'll have your money, and you'll be free of *So Perfect*."

"I'm 'Gwendolyn' again? Not 'Ms. Golden?'"

"I'll call you whatever you want, as long as you cooperate."

"What if I've changed my mind? Stuart looks like he's about to visit the queen, and no one has offered me so much as a powder puff."

In my *So Perfect* days, Armand always worked with Wardrobe to choose my outfits. He made sure that they were tailored, pressed, and ready for me to step into. He had opinions about my nails, hair, and makeup, and I trusted his judgment and went along. I don't know how to make myself look good, but at least I realize that I shouldn't go on television the way I look right now.

"Your choices were to do the interview, in which case you'd get your stock options and become free of your contract, or to refuse to do the interview, in which case we would sue you. You picked the former and it's too late to change your mind. We're almost ready to start shooting, in case you hadn't noticed. As for your personal appearance, you should've asked Armand to come and get you ready if you're incapable of doing it yourself."

I've overhead enough conversations today to know that Trey is angry at Armand's agent Josie, who has cut Trey out of the loop and is trying to free Armand of his *So Perfect* contract. Without Armand, there is no *So Perfect*, and Trey has nothing.

"Why do you want me to do this?" I ask, trying not to cry. I know I made the wrong choice. I know I'm stepping into a trap.

"It's not about what *I* want. The public wants more of you, Gwendolyn," he says. As if I'm toilet paper or batteries and there's a big storm coming.

I consider calling Smith. He has helped me so much since I came to town; I feel like he can fix practically anything that's broken. He certainly doesn't owe me, though. He just keeps doing kind things for me, and I keep allowing him to. I learned through Caroline that he wouldn't accept a commission on the house sale so that she could keep more money. Although I don't think the few thousand dollars was going to make much of a difference to him, I hate knowing he's been giving his time to me, literally for nothing. He also stored all my things from the Scenic house and had it delivered this morning, in addition to bringing lunch over himself. He has been a moral support and friend to me, and how have I repaid him? I haven't. I can't ask him to do more.

I know Walter Owens would run right over, if he isn't already standing outside one of the windows, peeking in. He took it upon himself to throw me a surprise going away dinner last night at the hotel restaurant. It was as awkward and presumptuous as his gift-bearing visit here this afternoon. Everyone says how sweet Walter is, but if he doesn't want me to take out a restraining order, he seriously needs to dial it back.

I found myself wishing that Smith were there last night instead of Walter. Actually, instead of Megan and Kyle, too. Megan was passive-aggressive towards Kyle, while he seemed irritated with her at every turn. He wasn't a bully so much as a nag. I can see that he's handsome, and he's clearly the competent, responsible one in their household when it comes to parenting, but I've come to the conclusion that Kyle's a whiny brat.

"Thanks for the lead on the house," I told him last night.

He glanced at Megan then frowned down at his plate.

"Nice and neat how that all worked out, huh?" Megan asked in a strained voice.

Kyle pouted and clanked his silverware. He got upset when a photographer appeared out of nowhere and snapped pictures of our table—which seems to always happen to me when Walter knows my plans.

Kyle and Megan left early, and Walter excused himself to take care of a hotel issue, leaving just my dad and me at the table. My dad pointed out that Kyle has never once held a real job. "Deadbeat," he called him, not for the first time.

"And who would be good enough for Megan, Dad?"

"Lots of boys she went to school with would have been good choices," he said.

"Boys from our neighborhood, who belonged to the country club, and attended Riveredge Academy, right?"

"Why not?" he asked.

"I wish Smith were here tonight," I said, trying to sound matter-of-fact.

"The realtor?"

My friend, adolescent love, a man I trust and think about almost constantly these days...

"Yes. The realtor."

"You still like him, all scarred up like that?"

"I don't notice the scars much," I said. It's true.

My dad seemed to really think about this, which struck me

because he's more of a talker than a quiet thinker. There aren't a lot of lengthy pauses during discussions with my dad.

"Your mom would've wanted to hear that," he said finally.

"Why? She hated Smith."

"I don't know. She was really sad when he had that accident. It shook her up. She was sick at the time herself. I think she'd like to know that people could look past his injuries."

The idea of my mother suddenly developing empathy so close to the end of her life seemed like a nice fairy story, but only about as real as one. If she'd cared about Smith's accident, she would've told me about it. Someone should have.

"Well, then I missed another chance to make Mother happy, didn't I?" I asked, patting my dad's hand.

My dad looked around like he was suddenly worried. He spoke low. "A woman called me up today, Gwennie. A reporter who said she was getting ready for your interview."

"I'm sorry anyone bugged you, Dad," I said. I kissed his cheek, hoping to erase the frown lines around his eyes. "It must suck to have me for a kid these days."

"I'm proud of you, Dedo. And I love you. I just hope you know that, and remember it. Your mom loved you very much, too. We may have made mistakes along the way, I know we did, but we never meant to hurt anyone." My dad's voice broke a little.

"What's wrong?"

"I miss your mom, I worry about your sister and you, and I'm just tired out. I think I'd better get on home."

I walked my dad to his car and took the back elevator up to avoid Walter Owens.

"Are we set?" Stuart Bolder asks as he gets his already-perfect makeup retouched. I try to ignore him and his entourage. No one offers me any makeup, and no one touches my hair. No one tells me to turn my chair, "a little more to the left. No, too much. Yes, *perfect*," like they do Stuart.

I know it's too late for any of that. We're about to start taping.

My muscles ache from unpacking boxes all morning. A hot shower would be just the thing. Caroline was so sweet to leave me with a practical welcome gift: a shower curtain, towels, and a bath mat for my master bathroom. She said we forgot to order them. I wouldn't have noticed until I'd gone up to shower, but Caroline thinks of everything.

In the show house, my bathroom had been—and this is no exaggeration because Armand told me himself when he measured—bigger than my bedroom here. My bedroom there was the size of the entire upper floor here. I don't mind that everything is smaller in this house, I just wish it were pretty, and cozy, like it was when it belonged to Caroline. It looks abandoned now, and as disheveled as me.

I tuck my feet up under my butt, take a deep breath, and try to relax. I have so many misgivings about this interview. I wish I was prepared, but I don't think normal rules apply to this tabloid/coliseum/circus world where I find myself hiding behind dark glasses/battling to the death/spinning overhead without a safety net. I'm beginning to think there are only wrong answers and the best I can hope to do is pick the least wrong among them.

Before *So Perfect* happened to me, I had never considered fame at all. I hadn't thought about riding high or plummeting, and I assumed every public figure went into their area of adulation or villainy with their eyes wide open. If I'd thought of it at all, I might have surmised that those celebrities who were unceremoniously toppled from their pedestals deserved it, and that the bad simply went along with the good. Over the past few years I've come to realize that some of us are clueless about the ramifications of what it means to become public property, that every mistake seems bigger when looked at under a tabloid microscope, that personal details it would be impolite to discuss regarding neighbors are unapologetically consumed about celebrities in checkout lines or on television talk shows. It's truly an awful bubble to be stuck inside. I don't know if this interview will burst it and set me free, or just blow me around some more.

The tension heightens as the hair and makeup people dash away, and Stuart Bolder is told we're on in five, four, three, two…

I frown and look off camera. I forget to breathe. I have no clue what to say—every line used to be fed to me. I've never done an interview without preparation. I've talked on camera about cakes and centerpieces and the perfect Valentines wine, but I've never had to defend myself against allegations that I'm a liar who deserves what she got.

I forget the specifics of the most recent insulting question when I turn back to Stuart. I answer the same way I did last time, and think maybe I'll just keep repeating the line over and over again, until they give up and leave me alone. "I was told that I had to do this interview to comply with the terms of my contract. I really don't have anything to say."

I wish my tone was tougher. I feel red patches form on my cheeks and work their way down to my neck and chest, like frost forming on a window, or mud colored dye soaking into white fabric.

Stuart smiles indulgently, as if I just complimented his tie. "How does it feel to have gone from riches to rags?"

"The 'riches' weren't really mine, and I don't consider this to be 'rags.'"

"Let's turn our attention to Armand Leopold for a second. Shall we?"

Footage of Armand laughing at my incompetence plays on a monitor beside us.

"I know that was edited to make Armand look bad," I say.

"Viewers all across the country thought he looked great!" Stuart laughs.

"To make me look bad then," I say quietly.

Stuart smiles into the camera, as if his whole life is one big audition. "Can you tell us more about the man everyone is uncharitably calling Scar Face, and your new love interest, hotel manager Walter Owens?"

"There is so much wrong with that question, I don't even know where to begin," I tell him wearily.

Stuart's laugh is brimming with condescension. "Well, I've found it's always best to begin at the beginning. Like *first* you learn how to cook, and *then* you might eventually pass yourself off as a chef. *First* you learn to decorate a house, and *then* you might call yourself a designer…"

"Fine, you jerk. First of all, I'd been trying to get out of my contract forever, but *So Perfect* wouldn't let me, and they knew from the beginning I wasn't anything they claimed. I'm only a painter."

Stuart tries to interrupt, but I steamroll over him. "Second, you called my friend a name which is very hurtful, not to mention tediously unoriginal. He was in a car accident, which could happen to any of us. And he's fifty times more attractive a man than you'll ever be, you ass! Third, though I have never dated and *will never* date Walter Owens, he runs a great hotel. If anyone out there is coming to town, I highly recommend the Riveredge on Main. He'll treat you well."

Stuart's smile seems to imply he's having a cozy scotch with a friend, not that I just insulted him repeatedly and gave some free advertising to my stalker. We all look up suddenly because someone is pounding at my door. Trey swears and an intern reluctantly opens up.

It's Smith! Seeing him helps me gather the rest of my courage.

I turn to Stuart. "You know what? Get the hell out of here." I take off my microphone and hand it to someone on his team. "All of you! I'm done with this interview."

"Oh no you're not," Trey says as he rushes over to me, not stopping until he's right in my face.

"Yes I am. Leave my house."

"You heard her," Smith says.

A cameraman comes in close and bumps into Smith's cane. I can't tell if it was on purpose. Smith staggers but regains his footing. Stuart chuckles like it's all a big joke.

"I told you all to leave my house!" I say.

"We'll get the police over here if you don't do as the lady asks," Taylor says.

Stuart throws up his arms and turns to Trey. "Lady?" he scoffs. "People are only interested in Armand now. I don't understand why we're going through all this trouble for an interview with this used paintbrush."

"What did you call her?" Smith asks, his voice unnaturally low.

"A used paint—," Stuart starts to repeat, but he doesn't quite insult me again before Smith punches him in the eye.

I'm jubilant for a fleeting moment. Then I see Smith lose his balance and topple over slowly, like a tree.

chapter sixteen

caroline

"Welcome home!"

I push open the door and the kids run in ahead of me. I left all the lights on for this homecoming. I hope they love it. I need them to love it.

"Wow, mom."

June turns back to me with bright eyes, and she's smiling. I exhale.

Joy and James walk through cautiously, like they're afraid to touch anything. They're smiling, too. They hold hands as they always do when something is new or exciting, or when they're tired. Or at the end of the school day after they have been apart for too long in their separate classrooms, which is still a big adjustment for two little people who had previously spent just about every sentient moment of their lives together, and even before. Witnessing their unquestioned trust in each other is one of the constant wonders of my life. I can't believe Blake could simply walk away from that.

I made this house as much like our old one as I could. It cost half what Gwendolyn paid for mine, and since the same bank was foreclosing on both, it approved the sales. I was able to get decent financing, preserve my precarious credit along with Blake's, and set aside his portion of the profits in an account. I'll be damned if he can say I owe him anything when all is said and done.

"This house is a lot smaller than our old one, which makes me happy because we'll be able to see and hear each other easier," I say.

I instantly second guess myself. Maybe I shouldn't shine a light on the fact that the place is tiny. I tend to point out all my imperfections. Suzie says that perhaps no one would notice that the foot of my gravy bowl has been broken and glued, or there's a hole under the arm of my good coat, if I didn't insist on telling.

Joy and James jump up and down; apparently they like the idea of a smaller house.

"Let's go upstairs!" James pulls Joy along. Neither of them would go upstairs alone in our old home, which wasn't huge by any means. It's true that we all tend to stick together, especially since Blake left.

"How many people live in our old house now?" James asks, turning back halfway up.

"One!" I tell him with my eyebrows raised, like it's so strange.

"Is she a giant?" he asks.

"Nope. She's a regular person."

A month ago I had such a different view of Gwendolyn Golden. I don't think I realized she was a real, flesh and blood woman, with fears, and worries, and problems, and dreams. She looked like she had it all, and it was all good. It's troubling to see how she is portrayed in the media now, when I know for a fact that she's practically the opposite. It makes me look at every celebrity differently than I used to.

"Is this house bigger or smaller than the house you grew up in, Mom?" Joy asks as she and James make their way down the stairs again.

"I think this is bigger," I say, reaching down to stroke her soft curls when she gets to the bottom.

I know it's bigger. The house I grew up in burned five years ago, and I'm sure the empty lot looks better than the house ever did. I like that Joy asked me this; it certainly puts things into perspective. This house is grand compared to the one where I lived when I was her age.

"And the one we just moved from was even bigger yet! I hope that regular lady doesn't get lost in there," Joy says before she and James run back up the stairs again.

I think of Gwen at the old, emptied-out house. I have to remind myself that she's a grown woman, that it's not my job to worry about her.

Because I wanted to keep things intact for the kids, I started taking the house apart yesterday when they left for school. I made several trips in my minivan with breakables, and the children spent the night at Suzie's so they wouldn't see everything torn asunder.

Yesterday afternoon as I carried out my last box of dishes, a stranger with a notepad got out of her car and came toward me quickly.

"Can I ask you a few questions?" she'd said.

She had black rectangular glasses and was dressed, from trench coat to shoes, in flat beige like the dead grass patches where snow had thawed on the lawn. She had a closed-off edge to her that stood out in our small Midwestern town, like a cappuccino machine in a cornfield. I wondered what she had already written on her notepad, and what she thought she could possibly add to it by talking to me.

"No you may not."

"What's Gwendolyn Golden really like?" she asked, standing close to me now.

"She's very sweet," I said, though I'd told myself I wouldn't say anything. Then I hurried away from the woman, as if she was contaminated just by virtue of her job.

This morning the moving van and hired brawn brought all our heavy things the quarter mile to this house. With the kids at school again today, Suzie was my assistant as we directed the movers, hung all the pictures, made up the beds, and tried to make it feel like home.

"Do you think she'll get lost in there, Mom?" Joy asks, having appeared again beside me.

"I think she'll be okay. She's a big girl."

"But not a giant," James adds.

My kids all have Blake's dark hair and eyes, with incredible long, curly eyelashes. I could stare at these children all day long.

"Faces and hands, then teeth brushing in your new bathroom, then stories, and then…"

"Eat candy?" they ask, nearly in unison.

Listing out the tasks ahead is a habit we started forever ago. The kids' job is to come up with some funny alternative to what really needs to happen. It's usually June who thinks of it, but the twins jump on board if they can.

"*No*, then a trip to Disney Land," I say.

"No! *Bed!*" Joy and James pretend they're setting me straight. They never get sick of this game.

I know someday they will, though. Someday they might also decide it's not necessarily a benefit to live in a house so small that we can always see and hear each other. They may one day also think it's odd that their mom saves all their old artwork, and has three levels of backup for every photo and video of them, like she would make time stand still if only she could.

So I remind myself to enjoy this moment, every moment, while it lasts.

I have logged so many hours here already, and touched every inch of every room, either with a sponge, rag, broom, mop, sanding machine, or paintbrush, or some combination of the above, that there really aren't any surprises left for me. At least not until I tackle the back yard.

I expected the kids to have a harder time adjusting to the newness. I thought they'd call me upstairs a few times to reassure them about new shadows coming from different streetlights than they're used to, or a toilet flush that sounds slightly more or less rumbly than the toilets sounded in the old house.

They climbed straight into their beds, though. I was able to orient them like they were in the old house. I also painted their rooms the same colors they'd gotten used to, and utilized all the same linens, pictures, and rugs. When I kissed the kids good night they said the house felt like home.

Their bedrooms are so tiny here I had to put dressers inside closets. I removed the closet doors and hardware and stored them above the rafters in the garage. We were heavily furnished in our old house, and moving into this smaller space meant I had to get rid of all but the most essential furniture pieces.

Gwendolyn was happy to buy what I couldn't use, but I almost wish she hadn't. The painted chairs, shelves, and odd little items that had made so much sense as part of a whole just looked sad and lonely in the bare house when I left. Like streamers after a party, swaying in an empty hall.

I stretch my legs out over the ottoman, and rest my back more comfortably against the couch. Our new little family room is at the rear of the house, with windows facing the back yard. When it's cleaned up it may even be better than our old one, because it leads to common land, so there are trees to look at instead of the back of someone else's house.

I chose this moss green chenille sofa with down pillows when Gwendolyn Golden said on television that a high quality sofa was the most important furniture item one could buy, and it was worth the money. I now know she was only saying what someone else wrote down for her. The poor thing is getting a couch that will arrive in two pieces through the mail! I smooth the soft chenille arm with my hand and think that this sofa has held up well, especially considering what it has been through: coffee and grape juice spills, three kids climbing and jumping on it, and today's move.

This sofa was a big splurge. I waited until it went on clearance, but it still cost a lot. I bought it back when perfection seemed attainable, when trying for it seemed to matter. In this little house that I have painstakingly made my own, the first time I've ever done such a thing without someone else's bank account at hand, or following someone else's instructions, I feel like I've come a long way.

It has been an endless few weeks, and I'm spent. I thoroughly expect another blink night when my head hits the pillow. I lean back and try to enjoy how my body feels in a silent, inert state. I shake my head and smile, because resting seems so alien. I've been running, and scrubbing, and lifting, and hammering for so long, it feels bizarre to simply sit.

I retrieve the stack of mail on the counter that I brought from the other house this morning. I sort the junk mail from the bills before I take the newspaper out of its plastic bag and open it up.

I'm soon sucked into a poorly written article about Gwendolyn. It includes a few pictures, one of which is a family portrait. I look at the faces, but they're a bit blurred.

It's sort of interesting to see Gwendolyn's dad. He looks curmudgeonly and wizened. Gwendolyn is a few inches taller than him, and much taller than her sister, who doesn't look anything at all like Gwendolyn. The woman resembles me far more than her famous sister.

I stop and look closer. I catch my breath and my heartbeat starts to pound in my ears as I study the photograph and read the caption. Megan Draves is Gwendolyn's sister's name. Her husband stands next to her, and in front of the group are their two children.

I can't believe it. I don't want to believe it.

Megan's husband looks so familiar I can practically hear his voice. I sigh deeply as I picture his intense eyes, and remember the smell of his cologne, like clean earth and leaves. Memories wash over me that I've alternately tried to banish and conjure since the day they were formed. I feel the softness of his dark chest hair under my cheek, his hand lazily caressing my back. He dozes beneath me while I listen for the church bell on the corner to say that it's time for me to go or I'll be late to meet the school bus. I hear him ask, "Can't you stay a little longer?"

For years Kyle had been a regular patron in the university library where I work, half an hour's drive from Riveredge. He was ambling toward a Master's in Education and asked me several reference questions over the years. I helped him find his answers, like I helped everyone else. Though he seemed to invite it, I never flirted with Kyle.

Not until I realized my husband was a cheat.

My face burns with shame and regret, and with a touch of longing, too. I think I'd been looking for validation that I was desirable, along with distraction from my anger, and maybe some revenge. I only visited Kyle's place three times before breaking it off. I thought at first I wanted to hurt Blake the way he'd hurt me, but I soon realized I didn't really want to stoop that low.

Kyle still calls, though I have repeatedly told him not to. I don't answer anymore. I want to forget about him.

Kyle had charmed me in ways I don't think anyone else ever had. Something felt a little off about him, though. Certainly not his lovemaking, but something else. It seemed strange that he was in his mid-thirties but didn't have a job, and still lived the life of a graduate student in his spare studio apartment. There were obvious reasons to walk away from Kyle: I'm married, and even though my husband has relinquished his claim on my loyalties, we still have three children together.

There were plenty of reasons to stop seeing Kyle, but looking at the photo in the paper, I realize that I didn't know the half of them.

chapter seventeen

smith

I try to ignore the reporter shivering on my front step. I wish she'd move on.

I wish a lot of things. I wish I had somehow managed to rescue Gwen last night instead of merely landing myself in the middle of her *Riches to Rags* story (which I wish wasn't being called that). I wish I hadn't blackened an eye and earned myself the promise of a very public lawsuit. I wish the whole surreal, made-for-TV fiasco would blow over, along with the bitter cold front that swept in last night and has settled deep into all my aches and pains.

It's my physical therapy morning, which is a lucky break for me. If I ever needed to see Irene, it's today. I call her cell phone.

"Can you meet me outside the hospital with a wheelchair?" I ask.

"Why? Are you okay?"

"I'm just a little rusty; it must be the weather. Hopefully you can get me oiled up like the old tin man that I am."

"I'll be waiting for you."

If I were a soldier I'd want Irene alongside me. I first met her after the frightening aftermath of my accident had passed, when my internal injuries had been stabilized, my broken bones had been set, and I knew I would at least live. With one leg basically crushed, and broken bones in one arm, six fingers, and I would have to look back at the records to know how many ribs, I thought physical therapy would ramp up slowly. But Irene made me focus on what I could do, not what I couldn't. She started working me the first time we met—working me *hard*. In a lifetime of challenges, I had never been challenged quite like that. I swore at Irene. I shouted. She was tough, upbeat, and dedicated. Ruthless, too.

"I'll get you out of that chair," she told me, "but only if you're willing to work like you've never worked before."

Two months later I was walking, such as it is. But there's a limit to what even Irene can do, and I have learned more about my own limitations since the accident than I ever wanted to know. I'll never walk any better than this, no matter how hard I work. The challenge now is to keep what I've gained and try not to backslide.

Safely arrived at the hospital, Irene makes it over to my car before I can even get out.

"I see this town has another superstar," she says as I transfer into the chair.

"Please, let's not talk about it," I reply in a low moan as she wheels me toward the building.

My feelings about last night are all over the map. I'm glad we were there to help Gwen put an end to that hatchet job of an interview. Though I hate to lie even by omission, and the truth about my accident hangs over my head like a grand piano ten floors up, I couldn't let Gwen learn it on camera from someone like Stuart Bolder. I enjoyed hitting the obnoxious, dimpled, metaphorical stand-in for every person who's ever insulted Gwen, and perhaps me. I hated falling to the floor as a result. I know I would've loved seeing Taylor physically throw all the vultures out, if I hadn't had to do it from my low vantage point.

When it was all said and done, it wasn't like I got to sweep Gwen into my arms and carry her up the stairs or anything. Once I fell, I had trouble getting up again. Taylor had to help me into a tortuous wooden chair while I tore at my coat looking for pain pills. I would have let him piggyback me to the car if Gwen wasn't watching. As it was, I had to wait twenty minutes until I could stand up and lean on my cane on one side, knowing Taylor would catch me on the other if necessary.

"I pulled something last night, Irene."

"Certainly not a punch, if what I read in the paper is true. And here I thought you were a nice guy."

She's making light, but I watch her face while we wait for someone to enter the PT suite ahead of us, and it's set like we're under fire. I think Irene appreciates the fragileness of my body even more than I do sometimes. I hadn't been really worried until I saw her expression.

"It's on the back of my good leg, below the knee."

Her forehead relaxes a bit. "Probably just a muscle. We'll check it out."

"It's okay to say it hurts," Irene tells me forty minutes later as she monitors the progress of one of the worst exercises. Sweat drips down my face and I want to scream. I'm afraid if I cry out, though, I might never stop. My leg is a crumpled shambles of collapsed nerves and misfiring signals. After years spent living with my amended self I can look at the damage without wincing, but I know it was worse when it was new to me. Being called Scar Face has been a reminder of how strangers see my body.

"How much longer?" I ask. I don't want to say it hurts. I've never liked admitting something hurts.

Irene pulls my leg straight and massages all the painful parts.

"Let me get the knots out and you'll be all done for today, Smith. Your pulled muscle will heal up just fine, but don't do any more crazy heroics to impress your girlfriend."

I try to smile, but can't quite manage. I hate my goddamn limitations.

"You don't believe she's my girlfriend," I say, sounding as defeated as I feel.

"Isn't she?" Irene looks at me in a way that I find surprising. I remember women looking at me this way, but only before the accident.

Sometimes I think there's a chance for Gwen and I, and other times it just seems impossible that she would go out with Scar Face if he ever gathered up the nerve to ask. "We're just old friends," I say.

"Well, in that case, I wondered if you wanted to come with me to the hospital fundraiser on the fifth. It's next Friday." She seems suddenly shy.

I don't know what to say. Irene is very pretty. She's kind. She pushes me to make the best of what I've got left. She has asked me out several times since I've known her, but I never thought she meant it. I assumed she was being sweet, being a friend. Today I can tell that she really wants me to say yes.

Before Gwen came to town, I would have jumped at Irene's offers if I had thought that she meant them. I can see that she's blushing; the scalp of her parted platinum blonde hair is pink. I haven't been on a date since the accident, and for several months before that. I'm not even sure how long it's been. Irene looks up and bites her lip.

"You really want me to?" I ask.

"I wouldn't ask if I didn't."

"Do you get bonus points for bringing a patient or something?"

"If you don't want to go, don't torture me, just say no."

"*Me* torture *you*?"

We both laugh. She takes an envelope out of her pocket and hands it to me.

"Here are the details. I wrote my address on there, too. Are we on?"

"I'd be honored."

I'm surprised to see Gwen and my mom seated together near the enormous stone fireplace in the senior community clubhouse. It's not shocking that they're both here: my mother lives in the complex, and Gwen spends a lot of time visiting her dad. Here she can escape unwanted attention because it's gated, and none of the residents would dare bother Gordy Golden's kid. They look up together and notice me.

Gwen smiles and my first thought is that she should wear green every single day because she looks so gorgeous in her emerald sweater. My second thought is that she's studying me too closely, like she's trying to figure something out.

I wish I could slow to a dramatic stop, suddenly drop my cane, do a forward roll, and pop up again like Gene Wilder as Willy Wonka. But I can't. Gwen comes to meet me and holds my right arm casually as we go forward.

"I've been tracking you down. Jessie said you had physical therapy this morning. I waited at your office because she thought you'd be back, but you never showed."

"How many autographs did she get you to sign?"

Gwen shakes her head, and I bet it was a lot.

"Your cleaner gave me quite a lecture," she says. I picture Shirley with her mop in one hand and the other on her plump hip.

"I'm sorry."

"She's a big fan of Armand. I promised I'd get her an autographed picture. She said you usually have lunch with your mom on Fridays, so I thought I'd look for you here."

I don't explain where I went after my therapy appointment. I had to visit my attorney because of the very expensive lawsuit that will be filed against me. I know it'll upset Gwen when she finds out. It upsets me, too. Throw Taylor's suit in and it's a goddamn double whammy, and not exactly my idea of a good way to spend part of a business day.

"Want to join us for lunch?" I ask.

"I wish I could, but my dad's expecting me soon. He's making pasta."

"What were you two chatting about?" I ask, looking from my mom to Gwen. I don't like the guilty look on my mother's face.

"We were talking about your accident."

I turn away for a moment and look out the window at the snow piled high along the parking lot's edges. I don't like to think about the accident, especially when I'm already in pain. I sometimes break out in a cold sweat and feel the aftershocks of the impact all over again. I wish they had been talking about my nice house, or my recent impressive sale of the 404 building.

"It must have been terrifying," Gwen says, putting her hand over mine. I feel the cuff of her soft green sweater touch my wrist.

On the night of the accident I had told myself I couldn't leave until I'd caught up on paperwork. It had been very late by the time I turned out the lights and locked the doors. Downtown had been practically deserted when I finally stepped outside into the cool, crisp night.

I had noticed a small group leave Coach's Bar three blocks up. Their distant conversation and laughter had grown quieter as they passed between the buildings until I heard the small metallic claps of their car doors shutting. I was in the middle of the lane by then, crossing to my car parallel parked in front of the Good Morning Café. I saw a white Suburban barreling up the street toward me. I had been momentarily confused because the stoplight between us was red; I'd been careful to cross according to the rules.

I realized the SUV was coming too fast to stop.

I remember lifting my heavy briefcase higher as I turned to face the Suburban head on. I knew I had no time to react, that it would be as futile as trying to outrun a sunset, though somehow time also seemed to slow sickeningly, too.

I don't think an impact like that can really be described with any success, certainly not by me. I only know that I'd give just about anything to erase the event so that I had never felt it, never experienced it. If I had been ten seconds later or earlier finishing my paperwork and crossing Main Street, I'd still be whole. Human bodies aren't made to withstand that sort of crushing insanity.

I fell. The SUV kept going.

I had been able to use my right arm and leg to crawl over to the sidewalk. I pressed 911 into my phone, which had been spared. I don't remember the conversation. I passed out before the ambulance arrived.

Siler was on duty that night and arrived in a squad car. Jones came to the scene as a volunteer fireman. Taylor was still a student at the university and didn't get the news until they knew I'd pull through. I'm often thankful for the fact that he didn't make the long drive home not knowing.

I had recognized the driver of the SUV. I had seen the

face freeze with terror as the realization of what was about to happen hit, too late to stop or change course, but not too late to understand. I have never, not for a minute, doubted that it was an accident.

Accident: such a minor word sometimes. A child wets his pants, a jar of pickles falls and shatters on a clean kitchen floor, a guy slips and lands on his ass while his friends laugh.

Accident: such an utterly devastating word sometimes.

Gwen's hazel eyes, so big when she's worked up about something, are made more vibrant by her sweater today. I pull my attention from them to look at my mom. Sternly. I honestly don't know if she's aware of who the driver was, but I don't think she'd tell if she knew. We protect each other in our family, and it was my choice to keep quiet. Still, this feels like dangerous territory.

I try to sound casual. "Well, I'm still here, alive and well, so it must not have been that bad. Hello, Mom." I reach over and pat her hand.

"I'm so sorry I brought it up," Gwen says, turning red.

Apparently my face must have betrayed some of my thoughts. I'm not nearly as good at keeping everything inside as I used to be. "It's no problem," I say.

She leans over and hugs me. It's a bit of an awkward embrace from our seated positions, but I don't mind.

"Thank you for last night, Smith. You were my hero, again. I don't know how I'll ever make it up to you," she says in my ear.

I think I could just stay like this forever.

After a moment she sits up and takes a reluctant look at her watch. "Oh. My dad's probably worried I'm not there yet. I'm glad I finally caught up with you! And I'll see you later. Okay?"

She gives my arm a pat as she passes behind my chair. "Oops. Someone dropped something," she says as she bends down and picks up Irene's invitation from the floor.

I had thrown away the envelope and it's just a single-sided piece of card stock. Gwen scans it.

"It's yours, Smith, must've fallen from your pocket." She hands it to me with a sad smile. She waves to my mom. We watch her walk out in her cowboy boots, which are woefully unsuited to Michigan winters.

My mom takes the invitation from my hand and reads it. There was never any pretense regarding privacy in our home growing up. If one of her boys received a letter, my mom had every right to read it. She used to search our pockets for cigarettes or joints, and I remember her actually frisking Siler as he left the house for months after finding a pint of whiskey in his jacket.

"Irene is your physical therapist?" she asks.

"Yup."

"But why would you go out with her when you're in love with Gwendolyn?" she asks, staring hard at me.

"You've been listening to your younger sons. They also believed the Lions would make it to the Super Bowl this year. How did that work out for them?"

"No, I've been watching you, Smith Walker."

I change the subject to get the upper hand. "Why were you talking about the accident, Mom?"

She fidgets with her bracelet. Her hands are age spotted and thin-skinned. She's gotten smaller and frailer over the years, and her hair has grown white. She looks suddenly very old to me, and I have a pang of fear that life is going by too fast. I'm afraid not only of her mortality, but mine as well.

"Gwendolyn said I must have been terrified when you got hurt, and so relieved when you came out of it okay. So I told her about it from my perspective."

"Gwen describes this sorry wreckage as 'coming out of it okay?'" I ask, meaning for it to be self-effacing, meaning to laugh a little.

My mom leans in and waits for me to look up. "Yes. And apparently this Irene woman would agree with her."

"Yes, Mom, I have to beat the women away. That's the real reason I use a cane."

She clutches my hand with a surprisingly strong grip.

"Life is short. Isn't it?" she asks.

I look at my aging mom, and think of my dad, a good and

kind man who died much too young. "Yes, it is. So?"

    "So live."

chapter eighteen

armand

Stuart Bolder wears his shiner like a merit badge and smiles like he's as innocent as a Girl Scout, but I'm not buying *any* of that man's cookies! I'm only watching him because my agent Josie called and said to turn on my TV and tune in to WJKS. I wish I hadn't, but then again, I can't turn away.

Stuart's got his best suit on and he's standing in the sunshine in front of the Grand Dame like he thinks he deserves to be there.

"What a night I had last night, folks! All you WJKS viewers out there know that it has been a spectacular fall from grace for Gwendolyn Golden. She had achieved moderate name recognition as a lifestyle guru when she lived with Armand Leopold in this *So Perfect* house on Third Street here in Scenic.

"Since then she was revealed to be nothing more than a fake with a penchant for setting kitchen fires. But now it seems as if the public is more interested in her than ever! Her erratic behavior last night during an interview conducted in her modest Riveredge, Michigan home has many wondering if she's lost more than her cushy *So Perfect* gig. Many are wondering if Gwendolyn Golden has lost her mind!"

I turn down the volume because I just can't listen to Stuart Bolder anymore. I'm ashamed I ever sat next to him on the sofa and made fun of Gwendolyn.

The small house that had been dolled up like a mini Grand Dame by my mini-me fills the screen. It's just a sad and empty bucket with all my savant's pretty things poured out. It calls to mind a newly-shaved head. The crooked picture hangers on the empty walls look like nasty little nicks and cuts.

I see they brought in lights for the interview, but they're as uneven as a teeter totter with my mama on one side and just about anyone else on the other. Stuart looks like he's taken some pointers from Barbara Walters; he's lit so softly he may as well be an angel. But when the camera pans the room, it looks bright and cold enough for surgery. They show Gwendolyn and I can't help but gasp. It looks like she's there for an interrogation.

I wouldn't have recognized her without the context, and that's really saying something, since I've seen her first thing in the morning about a thousand times. I could have flipped right past this channel and never guessed the washed-out woman sitting in an old wooden chair was my *So Perfect* partner.

Gwendolyn's eyes are at their slow loris-est. She looks genuinely ill in the harsh light. Much, much too thin. Don't even get me started on the hair!

A little montage like the ones news channels toss together for each crisis, as if they're really all the same anyway, from the human interest FIREMAN RESCUES OLD WOMAN'S CAT FROM TREE, to the grizzly train crash WILL COMMUTING EVER BE THE SAME?, to the soul-crushing mass shooting that'll make you cry your guts out TRAGEDY STRIKES AGAIN, IS YOUR TOWN NEXT?

There must be canned software to plug the new title in. In this case it says, GWENDOLYN GOLDEN: RICHES TO RAGS. They probably select from three or four music tracks with names like "heartwarming," "tragic," "outrageous," and "titillating," before they cram video snippets into place.

Gwendolyn's journey from beloved to bedraggled, beginning with her looking gorgeous (thanks to me) in a *So Perfect* cooking segment, a few seconds of her rushing with her head down behind old Chanel sunglasses into a cab at a Michigan airport, and a depressing scene of her looking like something the cat wouldn't bother dragging into her new house.

Josie calls again right after I turn it off. She and I are in synch.

"Did you see?" she asks.

"I saw enough."

"You could spend all day doing interviews if you like. We have lots of offers, starting with WJKS," Josie says.

I imagine the cute wardrobe guy, and getting gussied up. Then I think of Gwendolyn all sad and sorry in that empty house. I don't want to be on top if it means she's on the bottom. "No thanks."

"I agree," Josie says decisively. "We're in synch on that."

See?

"I sent you an email with a link to Gwendolyn's local paper. Read it first, then read the message I forwarded from Trey. Then talk it over with Gwendolyn if you like. Then call me."

I make her repeat her list so I can write it down and do it all. I love Josie's no-nonsense tone. I feel like she's Charlie and I'm an angel. I check my list, go to my laptop, and click on the email link to today's *Riveredge Daily* online.

> "According to trusted sources, Gwendolyn Golden only agreed to yesterday's interview taping in order to avoid being slapped with a lawsuit from *So Perfect*. *So Perfect* also promised to release Ms. Golden's stock options if she participated in the interview conducted by Stuart Bolder of WJKS North Carolina. The interview began in Ms. Golden's new home in the Hidden Pines subdivision here in Riveredge.
>
> *So Perfect* has not released her options, and they have indeed filed suit against her. For good measure, *So Perfect*, as well as Stuart Bolder, have stated they intend to file suit against local realtor and philanthropist Smith Walker. Sources allege Walker assaulted the interviewer, and, along with his brother Taylor Walker, forcibly evicted the interview crew from Gwendolyn Golden's home."

I look at my list and click on the message Josie forwarded from Trey. I don't know what to think. I decide I'd better call and talk it over with Gwendolyn.

"Hi Armand," she says.

My heart sinks because I think she might be crying. I don't want to picture Gwendolyn any uglier than she looked on the bits they salvaged from last night's taping. I really don't want to put a red nose on that image!

"Tell me all about it," I coax.

"So you can tell the rest of the world? No thanks."

Well, *Snap!* She's making me work for it.

"Okay, I admit I was a horse's rear last time, but today I could do twenty interviews and I'm turning them all down. I don't want to hurt you, kid."

"Thanks," she whispers.

I'd rather have her swearing up a storm like she usually does, instead of simmering in a sad little stew. I try to pull her out of it quick.

"So explain to me how the interview ended. That Scar Face guy came in and rescued you? Like Beast saving Beauty from the wolves?" I love that movie.

Gwen doesn't answer me so I try another way.

"So the guy's name is Smith, right? Tell me about him."

"He's a good friend."

"You said the two of you dated when you were kids. Was he in love with you back then?"

"I didn't think so."

"I bet he was. He obviously is now. My goodness is he a scary-looking character. But he's being sued for you, after all, so be kind."

She doesn't laugh, even a bit.

"What do you mean he's being sued?"

"I read about it in *your* local paper. If you're never going to read the news or watch TV, you should at least Google yourself once in a while to see how you're doing." I honestly don't know how she survives without a staff.

"What exactly did the newspaper say?"

"He's going to be sued. And his brother, I think. And you are, too."

"I know *I* am. I didn't know Smith was. God *damn* it! He

159

probably hates me."

I cringe and wait for the Lord to smite her like I always do when she cusses over the line. But he doesn't. To tell you the truth, I'm beginning to suspect He's not the best listener.

"I don't have any money and I don't want Smith dragged through any more crap for me. What am I going to do?" She sounds desperate.

"Well, did you happen to read your email from Trey?"

"No. How could that help?"

"I have my own copy right here, so let me go ahead and read it to you. The heading is pretty catchy: 'TO AVOID BEING SUED FOR BREACH OF CONTRACT.'"

"I'm already being sued. What more can he do to me?"

"Let's see. 'Armand Leopold and Gwendolyn Golden are both required to appear for an interview, to be conducted at the *So Perfect* show house on March 6. If you both comply, *So Perfect* will release your remaining company stock holdings immediately following the interview, and will drop all pending lawsuits against Gwendolyn Golden associated with the Riveredge incident.'"

Gwendolyn is so quiet, I'm not sure she's still there.

"Yoo-hoo?" I ask.

"I feel like this is a nightmare and maybe I'll wake up."

"You and me and the Grand Dame back together again? You call that a nightmare?"

"This might be one long party for you, Armand, but my friend is in trouble just because he stood up for me..." she doesn't finish. It sounds like she's crying again.

I try to be the voice of reason. "Listen Gwendolyn, if you'll do this I promise to hold your hand. I'll make sure you look at least as good as I do, or we'll take cyanide pills right afterward."

Again with the not laughing. I'm afraid the poor kid has starved the laugh cells right out of her body.

"Yoo-*hoo*?"

"I don't trust Trey. If I believed the lawsuit against Smith would be dropped, then I'd do it. I'd have to."

"Smith and his brother are both being sued, kid. Not just

from *So Perfect*, but Stuart Bolder also got in on the act."

"What?"

"Don't worry. Josie's entertainment attorney can fix everything, I bet. If I can get all the lawsuits dropped, will you do the interview?"

"If you got it in writing, then I'd have to. But it would have to be the last time, ever."

Alrighty then, my mind is racing right along. First things first: how to make Gwendolyn presentable in one short week?

"Is there a good spa in town?" I ask.

"So I can look nice as I'm led to slaughter?"

"We're not going to settle for nice. You'll look gorgeous, and we'll go down together if it comes to that. I'll find out where you need to go and make all your appointments for you. Just please remember to eat this week! I'm calling my agent to get everything in writing."

Is it so bad to admit that I still want my mother to accept me? I think I must have Post Traumatic Stress Disorder, and Battered Woman Syndrome, and Lost Cause Syndrome all rolled into one. Why do I care, when I know in my heart that the woman is just plain crazy?

Because she's still my mama.

She has called several times today but I haven't answered. I make myself pick up when she calls again.

"Hello, ma'am."

"Gladdy Prinster showed me your wife on TV. On YouTube."

"Gladdy Prinster again?"

"She just got elected leader of our prayer circle."

I picture it. I try to put it back out of my mind.

"How are things?" I ask, though I know there's never been much in my mama's life besides church. Except now evidently YouTube.

"Fine. We were talking in circle about what it's like to be on television. One person said she thought sometimes mothers would be in an audience, if her child was on a show."

"Gladdy Prinster?"

"I believe so."

"She said that, did she? Well, would you like to come to a big interview I'm going to do a week from tomorrow?" I don't know why I ask, but I do.

"Someone said that if a mother was to go to a show that her child was on, her child would send a ticket and get her a nice hotel."

"Gladdy Prinster might be right about that," I say.

"She's right about everything."

I know that isn't true, but I also know there's no sense arguing the point with my mama.

"I better go now, ma'am, I see my agent is trying to call me."

"Oh! You better answer."

"Trey and Stuart just pitched an idea they wanted me to run by you," Josie says. She always cuts to the chase.

"What's that?" I ask.

"They'd like to help you create a syndicated show, produced by WJKS." She doesn't sound either excited or skeptical. I think she's letting me lead. I love that.

"A decorating/cooking/lifestyle show with me as the superstar?" I ask, just to clarify. Plus I wanted to say the words out loud.

"It's only in the idea stage. I take it that you might be interested?"

"I might be," I say, trying to sound cool and casual, while inside I'm shrieking: *My own show? Is she kidding me?*

"I'll tell them it's worth gathering specifics. Then we'll all sit down and talk about it."

"Do you think they'd let me use the Grand Dame?" I ask.

"I don't know. Is it important to you?"

"Yes. I'd have to say it is."

There are many catch-your-breath beautiful old places in Scenic, in varying degrees of falling apart and being put back together, but the Grand Dame called to me from the moment I first saw her. I loved her before I ever even walked inside. She had such a pretty face, with tall windows on either side of her front door. Luckily no one had fought her age every step of the way, like a panic-stricken former Hollywood starlet slowly maiming herself one surgery at a time. The Grand Dame is an example of how it's not only possible to age well, but that aging can be a virtue. Every decision and change along the way has set her apart, and now she is unique in all the world.

"Would it be a deal breaker if you can't use the house?" Josie asks.

"An actual deal breaker? Maybe not," I say. It's actually pretty scary to think how bad the terms would have to be for me to say no to stardom.

"I'll give you a call when they have a proposal to review," Josie says.

"Tell Trey no focus groups are allowed!" I call out.

"Okay, you're the boss," Josie says.

I love the sound of that.

chapter nineteen

gwendolyn

I shut every blind to hide away, and switch on all the lights for company. Some rooms remain dark because they don't have overhead fixtures. Caroline helped me order lamps which might already be in the garage, stacked within the myriad UPS and FedEx packages. I don't have the mental energy to pull them inside and start assembling things, though. It takes a certain amount of optimism to open a box and I'm not quite there.

I put some pizza that I brought home from my dad's place into the microwave for forty seconds. Armand claims to be allergic to microwaved leftovers. He has rules about everything. Basically they come down to one overarching principle: however I do things is wrong. I thought his nitpicking ways were sort of endearing, that we had a mutually-beneficial, symbiotic thing going on. He likes to be great at everything, and I didn't mind letting him have his way. Maybe what he really enjoys about being around me is that my incompetence makes him feel awesome by contrast.

Cheese has melted onto the paper plate and I have to eat the droopy pizza with a fork because it flops when I try to pick it up. I miss Armand's cooking so much I could cry. He elevated every meal into a little masterpiece. I loved his food, and when it quieted down in the evenings after everyone went home for the day, I loved his warm and cozy home that looked, smelled, and felt amazing.

My dad's pasta lunch hadn't worked out. I was eating it out of politeness, but after a few bites he took my plate away and dumped the contents into the garbage along with his own. It was an easy choice for us to order in; my dad doesn't currently want to be seen in public any more than I do. It's depressing enough that I'm a pariah, but it sucks a thousand times worse to know I'm bringing my family and friends down with me.

This floppy slice is pretty gross, but it's better than starving. I haven't filled my fridge or pantry yet and now I don't know how I'll be able to do it. I can't simply go into the grocery store like a normal person. I'd probably be better off back in my lavender hotel room—and I do mean lavender. Walter had a lavender carpet put in while I still lived there, but at least he waited until I moved out to have the walls painted. He has doubled the rate for the room, which is now advertised as the Gwendolyn Golden Suite.

I throw away half my slice.

I can't seem to stop thinking about Smith. It was so chivalrous of him to come over here last night, but I don't know what possessed him to do it. How did he know I was in trouble and wanted help? It seems like there are always more questions between Smith and me than answers. The story his mom told me at the senior community clubhouse this morning was yet another example.

After mentioning that her boyfriend Caleb was taking her out to dinner at the Riveredge Country Club tonight, she said, "Smith still hates that place."

"Still?" I asked. I never knew he hated it there.

"It just always intimidated him so. He felt like a fish out of water. And then there was that awful night."

I suppose my expression told her that I didn't understand.

"You probably don't even remember that country club graduation dinner you invited him to. He was so nervous to spend time with your family."

"Is that why he stood me up?" I asked.

"Stood you up? No, you must be thinking of another boy on another night. The night I'm thinking of, Smith had worked all day at the 7-11 and got home with barely enough time to shower before he had to leave. I remember him running out to his old Impala and it wouldn't start. His dad was at the factory already and I didn't have a car myself, so Smith went next door and asked if he could use Brenda Closs's car to try and jump his.

"I remember hoping with all my might that the engine would catch, because I knew he thought the world of you. I was excited when the engine caught, and he left it running to make sure it wouldn't go dead again while he returned Brenda's car.

"Smith was dressed up so nicely and he'd bought you flowers that I'd seen him put carefully on the passenger seat. I remember thinking, 'he's going to be glad to leave us behind, and enjoy his scholarship down in North Carolina beside that Golden girl.'"

She looked around the clubhouse this morning when she paused in her story, like she was surprised to see it there because she'd been carried back in time by her memory. She took a sip of her coffee and asked me again if I wanted any. They always have fresh coffee and cookies at the clubhouse. I declined. Then she leaned in confidentially.

"Well, Smith was going to be a few minutes late to your dinner, but he was going to make it. As he was backing out of the driveway, though, a friend of his dad's was waiting to pull in. Smith saw before I did that something was wrong and he came back and parked the car.

"Smith's dad had collapsed at work. The friend had come to deliver the news in person. They'd called in an ambulance and he'd been rushed to the hospital. Siler, next in line after Smith, fed the other boys their dinner while Smith took me on to Riveredge Memorial. I hope you don't mind, but Smith gave his dad your flowers."

She had smiled weakly at me. I put my hand over hers and patted it gently. "I'm glad he did, Mrs. Walker. I would have wanted him to, had I known."

"I'm glad. Well, it was morning before we were back at home again. For a while there it looked like Smith's dad was going to rally. But it wasn't to be," she said, shaking her head.

"He sort of dwindled for a while before he died, like he was giving us all time to get reconciled to the idea. That was the kind of man he was. He didn't just act rashly, he took his time and made sure what he was going to do was the thing that needed to be done. I suppose death wasn't much different."

I patted her hand again, though I was confused by her story and couldn't quite reconcile it in my mind. She shook her head solemnly. "It's one thing to make your own sacrifices, but another thing altogether to have your own child making sacrifices for you. I think the weight of that is heavier when I see you, Gwendolyn. I know Smith wanted to follow you, honey. I'm sorry it didn't work out that way."

"I never knew about your husband," I said quietly.

"You didn't?" She seemed to wake totally from her memory at this.

"No. I left for a long trip the day after the dinner Smith missed at the club, the night your husband collapsed. I thought Smith had just stood me up." I sighed at the tragic absurdity of it. "I was gone for six weeks, so I didn't know your husband had died either."

"Smith must have mentioned it when he told you about the change in his college plans?"

"I didn't give him the chance. I was hurt he wasn't coming. I didn't know why, but I thought it was because he simply changed his mind. I always worried he didn't care for me as much as I cared for him."

"Well, I'm sorry you two didn't talk to each other honestly. Smith always thought very highly of you, Gwendolyn. Very highly."

I wish that I could be as certain of Smith's feelings as his mom seemed to be.

I'm a grown woman, Smith is a grown man. I don't have to pretend I'm married to Armand anymore, and I certainly don't have to hide him from my family. I could simply call him up.

He doesn't know the truth about next week's interview, though. I don't want him to find out that he's the main reason I agreed to do it. Armand's attorney advised me to take Trey's offer, and I've got it in writing that immediately following the interview, any lawsuits against Smith and his brother Taylor will be dropped. My lawsuit will be dropped too, and I'll be entitled to $100,000 in stock options that I'll cash out immediately. I'm afraid Smith might try to talk me out of it; he might try to play the hero again, no matter what it costs him.

I climb the stairs to the small bedroom where I moved all my art supplies. It doesn't have its own bathroom, an enormous stainless steel sink, or beautiful mullioned windows like the attic studio in Scenic. This is a simple, plain room, with only an easel, and me.

The associate professor I had loved for a year in college used to say that the most important first step in any artistic endeavor is framing your scene well. First you have to decide what you're trying to capture. Even with something as seemingly simple and obvious as a portrait, there are limitless options. You could choose to go in very, very close, and perhaps just frame a single eye. Or you could do a full body portrait that also captures the context of the room where the person stands. Or anything in between.

Since college I haven't been very cerebral about art. I try to tune out and let my hands do the thinking. I don't like to discuss it much, because like love, trying to articulate beauty only seems to water it down and make it flimsy. That was the philosophy of another art professor of mine. When anyone would start an existential conversation about the act of creation, he'd say, "For God's sake, just shut up and *work*!"

I look skeptically at my canvas and draw a meandering footpath.

By the time it registers that someone is pounding on my door, I get the impression it may have been going on a while. I haven't given any thought to household safety matters for four years. We had live-in help at the show house, the property was fenced, and there was an alarm system. My suite in Walter's hotel was located on the restricted top floor, well away from the comings and goings of the lobby. I feel vulnerable suddenly, realizing that Alejandra and Miguel aren't here, nor Armand, nor the hotel staff. It's down to me.

I see that it has grown dark outside as I set my palette on the floor. I take off my smock and hang it on edge of the open door, paint side out. I look at my jeans, which appear to be paint free. I try to see the seat of my pants to be certain, but after a few dog-chasing-her-tail rotations I decide I'm surely clean enough to peek out the window and see who's there.

Megan never visited me at the hotel. We have spent as little time together as possible since I've been in town. I open the door for her warily. She rushes in and slams, then locks it, as if all the runners in the New York City marathon are chasing her up the street and my doorway is the finish line.

As I look closely at my sister, I notice a few very odd things. First, she's not wearing a business suit, she's in what might be yoga wear. This is strange indeed. Second, she looks like she's been crying. That would mean she had feelings, so I'm justifiably skeptical.

I stare at her a minute before I have a sudden and terrifying thought.

"Dad?" I ask.

Megan shakes her head. Then she does something horrific.

I can't remember ever seeing her do anything like this, not at our mom's funeral, not when a boy broke up with her in high school or college, not when she fractured her arm attempting a new landing from the high bars.

Megan bursts into tears.

It's terrible to see a very mean person cry. It looks like anger. Normally when people cry in my presence, my instinct is to hug them, to pat them on the back, to softly say soothing things. Megan looks like she's viciously chewing air. I tell myself to go to her, but myself won't budge. I compromise by leaning in a bit and saying, "What the hell is *wrong* with you?"

Good. It made her stop.

"This place is hideous," she says.

I look around and sigh. "I know. But it was really cute when Caroline lived here. It's like she took all the personality with her when she left."

Somehow this exchange causes the horrible thing to happen again. This time, thank God, Megan hides her face in her hands. While I wait for her to stop, I survey the house some more. It's true that it looks like a pit now.

Megan resurfaces and I think of her children and her husband and become scared again. "Is anyone hurt?" I ask.

She shakes her head. "Caroline Penny," she says.

"What about her?" I ask, now worried for Caroline and her children. "Do you know her? Is *she* okay?"

"Kyle is having an affair with her," Megan says. She appears calmer and more lucid now, though I would have thought that if she'd have trouble saying anything, then that would be it.

"Your happy homemaker friend and my husband..." Megan dissolves into tears again.

I don't want it to be true. It makes my stomach hurt. I remember that Kyle mentioned this house to me the day I came back to town and Megan had sounded jealous when he did.

"Caroline is only the latest. Kyle has had three affairs in seven years."

"And you just found out about all of them?" I sit on the cold wooden floor and motion for Megan to take a chair, a painted wooden one that Caroline left. She just stares at it.

"No. I find out about one every few years. When it ends, he tells me all about it. It makes him feel better to get it off his chest."

"What an ass!" I feel sorry for Megan. No wonder she's such a bitch.

"He's really an amazing father. He really is. He takes care of the kids and I get to work whatever hours I want and know they're fine...I'm about as maternal as our mother was, which we both know isn't exactly the best way to raise kids. Kyle makes up for me. He's worth it."

"What's the problem then? Sounds like it's all going really well." I shake my head in horror, empathy, and sadness.

"Kyle says he's in love with her." Megan stares down at the floor a few feet in front of where I sit.

"He's not usually in love with them?"

"No!" she says, as if I've just insulted her.

Or him. I honestly have no idea what logic she's using, but she seems put out by the suggestion. There's a lot I could say here, but I'll only fight with my sister when she's a worthy opponent. Not now. Looking at Megan, I feel sort of nauseous, sort of curious, and suddenly very tired. I must've been painting for a long time because my arms feel heavy.

"Can you talk to her?" my sister asks, looking directly at me for the first time since she arrived.

"No!"

"Please, Gwen?"

"And what would I say?" I demand, with the whine Megan always seems to bring to my voice.

"Maybe tell her that I know about the affair, and that I don't want to lose my husband. And find out if she's in love with him. Okay?" Megan makes this pathetic request with what I can only guess is supposed to be an imploring smile. I turn away quickly.

"I suppose I can try," I say, though my heart sinks at the thought.

"I just can't lose him…"

I don't want to think about Megan and Kyle's home life. It sounds like they do more acting than Armand and I ever did.

When a painting fog comes over me, I tune out and lose track of time. I can't plan it or will it, I can only succumb to it if it happens. It's when I produce my best work. It's when I feel like a real artist.

It's nine o'clock and I'm ready to shower and sleep after I clean out my brushes. Megan thankfully left as soon as I agreed to speak with Caroline. I couldn't offer my sister a drink or a comfortable place to sit, though I doubt she would have taken either anyway.

I stop in the doorway of my makeshift studio and glimpse the side of the canvas that consumed the past five hours. It's turned away so that all I see are the colors: saffron, dandelion, verdigris, copper, vermillion, and chestnut. Cornflower, cyan, and azure at the top. Sky.

I walk around to see the entire canvas, a very large one. I cross my arms in front of me and narrow my eyes.

It's a strange process of discovery I sometimes experience, to see a painting that logic tells me I made with my own hands, but it feels somehow beyond me, too. Like how a writer in his eighties might feel perusing a manuscript he wrote in his twenties. For artists, moments of objectivity are as rare as they are essential. Sometimes heartbreaking, sometimes heart lifting, such an instance might test an artist's will, providing proof that critics are right, the work isn't special. Or it might be a godsend, giving a pivotal boost of confidence that is to an artist more important than bread or breath.

I smile at the canvas. This is not one of those elating or deflating times for me. It's just a simple discovery, an appreciation of the color, and movement, and energy that I put out there. I don't believe this painting proves that I'm a genius, but it also doesn't prove that I'm a hack. I like it.

I lean in and study details. The landscape I painted has a tree at its center. Though I hadn't deliberately dwelt on a specific one, I see that I know it. It's the beautiful old oak in Riveredge Park that I drew in pencil on a small sketchpad years ago. That piece has a youthful version of Smith and me drawn into the foreground; it now sits on Smith's wide oak mantle. I saw him put it there.

He'll like this painting, I think.

Then I remember all the havoc I've caused him: the stupid lawsuit, his barbaric nickname, reporters dogging him. I also think of a woman named Irene. Maybe he'll never see this canvas...

The thought makes me wince, especially when I look closer at the painting and find a hidden detail, something that both surprises me because I hadn't consciously thought to put it there, and touches me with the bittersweet rightness of its presence. Leaning against the tree, almost hidden in the expressive whorls of the trunk, is Smith's cane.

chapter twenty

caroline

I hear the phone ring as I enter the house through the garage. I kick off my boots and hang up my coat. Since I just put them on the school bus, I know the call can't be about my kids, so I don't hurry to see if someone left a message.

I'm distracted by a stack of framed pictures on a console table that barely fits in the mudroom. These were the ones that I couldn't, or perhaps didn't is a better word, manage to fit on the walls of this smaller house. The kids must have looked through them, because I know I had left one of my mom when she was younger on the top, where a photo of Blake and me in our early twenties now sits.

I look through a photo collage of candids that have faded because they'd been on a sunny wall in the old house. They're of our early marriage, when I was pregnant with June, and when she was small.

I have always loved motherhood, even pregnancy. Though morning sickness and heartburn were annoying, I never doubted that the result would be worth it. I wanted to be the best mother in the entire world. I wanted to be the kind of mother I'd wanted myself. I wanted to have the kind of house I'd wanted to come home to as a child. I wanted my kids to have a dad that would always love them, who would always be around.

Maybe I slept with Kyle because I was looking for a way to feel guilty. Guilty enough so that reconciling with Blake wouldn't be insane. I hoped that I'd have the opportunity, because Blake would come back. In my panicked mind, perhaps I thought that when he did, we would be even. There. All better. I didn't actually logic it out like that, but I'm afraid deep down that might be what I was going for.

I look through the pile of pictures and see Blake holding the twins for the first time; he's crying. I see June accepting a rose from him after her little ballet solo in first grade. I see the pink and blue tricycles Blake put together for Joy and James's fourth birthday, with big bows on them, like life would be one happy birthday after another.

I think of other moments that weren't captured by a camera, that now only exist in my mind. And perhaps his, though I can't be sure anymore. I remember Blake and me waiting together while my mom had emergency bypass surgery. I remember him racing home when I told him June had taken her first steps. I remember painting our house together, taking long drives, being in love.

I put the pictures down and walk away. I tell myself that it's too easy to think you need someone when you look at shared details, moments in life that were pivotal and indelible. I tell myself that I need to take a step back and try to see the big picture, and remember that Blake isn't in it any more.

My husband has consistently insisted that he never had an affair with his colleague Francine. He said I was always jealous of her, so he didn't mention the fact that she had also signed on for the project in Spain. Blake repeatedly said that Francine has a long-term boyfriend and that my accusations were unfair to everyone, not just him. I didn't believe it.

Yet I chose to believe that Kyle was unencumbered. Though I could've surmised there was more to his story, I didn't look closely enough to find out. I now know Kyle lied to me. I assume Blake did, but I'm not completely sure.

I fill the teakettle and turn on a burner before I remember to check for a phone message. The call I missed was Blake, saying that he's hoping to reach me as soon as possible, that there has been a slight change in his plans.

My face reddens and I delete his message. Of course he's not coming back; I should have known. I'm so glad I didn't tell the kids that their father would soon be home in Riveredge. That he'd be living close enough for them to see him often. That these six months of having him gone might be just a blip of a memory for them, not a potential weakening of the foundation that they'll need for building healthy, trusting personalities. Thank God I didn't take the lying bastard at his word.

I pull out my budget notebook and see that the quarterly piano lesson bill for all three kids, plus June's ballet tuition, are due soon. I hope that Blake will still pay for these. I'm afraid he's not only changing his mind about coming back to Riveredge, but has decided that since he didn't quite find himself in Spain, he needs to go further still. Like a pilgrimage to Tibet that requires him to actually quit his goddamn job.

I choose Enlightenment from the tea cupboard this morning. I'm pouring boiling water into my mug when I'm startled by a knock.

"Hi there," Gwendolyn says when I open the back door.

She's wearing a scarf and huge Jackie-O style sunglasses, as if there is anyone left in Riveredge Michigan who wouldn't recognize her from a mile away. She's wearing her trademark jeans, t-shirt, crocheted sweater, and cowboy boots. I saw in the supermarket how her daily ensemble breaks down, in a piece entitled: *How you can have golden girl style without the bad press.*

"I walked over, and cut through a few back yards because a reporter was parked in front of my house this morning," she says. I mentally trace her route, alongside fences, more visible and conspicuous than if a white-tailed deer stood on its hind legs and danced the can-can through the neighborhood.

"An acquaintance of mine, maybe you know Walter Owens from the Riveredge on Main? He brought these over and I wanted to share."

All I need is a little more cellulite to round out my self-esteem. I reluctantly take the bag of donuts she offers.

Gwendolyn removes her wet and snow-covered cowboy boots when I motion for her to come inside. I can't believe she chose to wear those completely non weatherproof $500 boots while cutting through Michigan back yards in February.

She takes off her giant sunglasses and studies the décor, as if it'll all be on a test.

"How did you make this house look so great, so fast? It's really gorgeous! I wish I could live here."

Her voice comes off a bit whiny, like the vending machine is jammed and she's dying for a Snickers bar. I consider answering thusly: *I thought, planned, scrubbed, painted, and worked my fingers to the bone. What do you think? I wiggled my nose and it all just happened, like you used to do?*

"Seriously Caroline. How?"

I sigh heavily and consider another option: *I'm sorry that I can't distill my entire hellacious experience of transforming this house from an unlivable fish cemetery to a family home into a sound bite that you can not only comprehend with very little effort, but replicate by snapping your fingers.*

I love the picture she drew of my kids, though, and I appreciate how flexible she was with the house transaction. I feel a surge of pride that she sees how hard I've worked and thinks the results are beautiful. I still want her to leave me to my "rags," though.

"I just worked hard at it. Hey, thanks for the donuts. I'd ask you to stay for tea, but I have to finish doing the laundry before I leave for work." *Plus I'm precariously low on Enlightenment.*

"I'm sorry I just appeared unannounced. I don't have a land line yet, and I misplaced my cell phone charger." She shrugs with a self-conscious half smile that annoys me because it makes her look so pretty.

"No problem. Thanks again for the donuts."

"I, uh, well I promised my sister I'd speak with you, so maybe we can get together tomorrow or something?"

My face flushes hot. I think Gwendolyn's is just as red as mine must be.

"I probably have ten minutes to spare," I say quietly.

"Okay. Um, do you remember Kyle?" Gwendolyn asks. She wrinkles her nose like she hates to say the words as much as I hate hearing them.

I take a deep breath and let it out. I consider running out the door in my socks. I consider eating the entire bag of donuts. I'm thankful that my kids are in school—overhearing this discussion would not make for good formative memories.

"Kyle is my sister's husband," Gwendolyn whispers like it's a confession of hers, not mine.

"He never told me he was married," I say. I hope it's the worst sentence I'll ever have to utter.

Gwendolyn motions to the table with her head cocked to the side, and I nod for her to sit down without moving toward it myself. She sits with one leg folded under her.

"I know it's none of my business, but in college I dated an associate professor for a year before I knew he was married. Some men are just such *asses*! I'm not asking what happened, and I actually don't want to know. I'm only here because I promised my sister Megan that I'd talk to you."

"Why? It ended months ago." I sit down across from Gwendolyn without really intending to.

"Kyle says he's in love with you."

My heart beats in my ears. "In love with me? I don't know how that's possible. I only saw him a few times. I broke it off months ago."

"Megan said he loves you. She's afraid he might leave her and the kids because of you."

A spaceship landing on the roof right now might actually make my life seem less strange.

"Pardon?"

While she repeats the aforementioned insanity I eat a chocolate-covered fry cake in four bites. Again I consider running out of the house, eating the whole bag—anything would be better than participating in this conversation.

"Apparently Kyle has had a lot of affairs. He must be pretty charming or whatever." Gwendolyn blushes anew and I want to sink into the floor. "Megan says he's a really great dad. Apparently she believes he's worth putting up with all his shit."

"This is ridiculous," I say, making a decision.

I grab the phone and stare at it, realizing I don't know the number. I memorized the number to his studio apartment near the university, but obviously he doesn't really live there. He said he doesn't carry a cell phone. He had a live-by-my-own-rules quality to him that pulled me in, partly because it felt like the opposite of Blake's button-down style. Even if Kyle is currently at his apartment, I don't want to call him there. When I hear his low husky voice I don't want to imagine him in that space, with the vaulted ceiling and exposed brick walls, and the bed behind him. I want to talk to him where his wife and kids live.

"You stand here while I do it," I say to Gwendolyn. "And please dial for me."

After three rings a woman answers. I take a deep breath. If Gwendolyn wasn't here staring with her huge eyes I'd hang up the phone.

"Um, hi. My name is Caroline."

"This is Megan."

"Uh, hi. Listen, I've spoken to Gwendolyn and I want you to know that I had no idea Kyle was married."

She doesn't reply. I can't blame her. What would I say in the same situation?

"I broke it off with him months ago. I don't return his calls. I wouldn't date him again even if he were single, if he won the Lotto, or for any reason."

"Would you mind telling him that?"

"I already have. But sure, I'll say it again."

"Hold on."

While I wait out one of the most profoundly awkward moments of my life, I look at the kids' artwork on the window to steady myself. I need to focus on why life, despite its present state of unreality, is inherently good.

"Hello?"

Somehow hearing Kyle's voice focuses all my anger. Not just from the past few days, or six months, but all of it, forever.

"I will never date you. I hope to never see your face again."

"Caroline…"

"And one more thing. You'd be wise to hold on to that wife and family of yours!"

I didn't mean to yell. I look up to see that Gwen's eyes have overtaken the vast majority of her face. I slam down the phone.

I never told Suzie about Kyle. I'm stubborn and I'm proud, and when I've been a complete idiot I don't run out and get a tattoo that commemorates my transgressions for all the world to see.

"How are those donuts?" Suzie asks when she passes through the door five minutes after I called her in tears. Leaving her winter boots on the rug, she comes and sits across from me at the table.

I laugh sort of hysterically, and then I start to cry. I've eaten three donuts. I push the bag over to her.

It's so good to be with someone solid and steady. I don't know if the fact that Suzie is ten years older than me makes her seem so wise, or if she was born that way. I would have been lost without her these past months, actually for my entire life. It takes me under five minutes to tell Suzie about my affair and its aftermath, including Gwendolyn's visit this morning.

"I feel sorry for Gwendolyn," she says.

"Because?"

"Because she and her sister don't get along, which is just plain wrong. Because she has become a joke to a lot of people. Because it must stink to be publicly dragged through the mud. I bet she could use a real friend," Suzie says.

"So *you* hang out with her then. I don't want to, she's a basket case."

"So were you a little while ago. And she helped bail you out."

I see the truth in Suzie's words, and take some pride in the fact that she thinks I've moved on from basket case status to someone who might actually be able to offer help. Even after what I just confessed to her, she still looks at me with love in her eyes.

Soon Suzie leaves so that I can get ready for work. She hugs me on her way out. "The kids are great, the house is great. You're doing good."

She's right, I tell myself. The house went from unlivable to welcoming because of me. My children have not only grown, but positively blossomed in my care. I can handle a lot more than I ever gave myself credit for.

Half an hour later I'm dressed, made up, and ready to leave for my shift at the library when the doorbell rings. I approach cautiously, hoping that it isn't the reporter I shooed away over the weekend.

The man on the other side of the door is at once very familiar, and somehow different. He's tan, his hair is longer than I've ever seen it, and he's trim. He looks at me through the glass and I don't know whether to open the door and fly into his arms, or to turn around and pretend he's not even there.

I barely recognize my husband.

chapter twenty-one

gwendolyn

My dad has been moody and distracted for days. I remember him as a cheerful guy growing up. He was always quick to tell a joke, especially when my mother was dour—which was most of the time. Maybe he was trying to make up for her, and now that she's gone he considers himself off the hook.

When he called and asked me to come over tonight, I should have said, *Sorry Dad, I'm in too much of a rush trying to get ready for tomorrow.* He seemed to really want me there, though, so I'm driving over through the drizzly darkness. I'll just have to pack my suitcase later.

Tomorrow is the big day. I'm not looking forward to it so much as I'm looking forward to having it over. I'm catching an early flight to North Carolina for the interview with Armand. I can't wait to put *So Perfect* behind me.

I was always uncomfortable with the name. The words "so perfect" mocked me. Whenever I saw them written down or heard them spoken, they already had the sarcastic edge that Stuart Bolder has adopted since the story broke. Armand thought of it, so I tried not to be critical or point out the irony. He bought in to the concept enough for both of us.

I'm nervous to walk into that house again, knowing that the cameras will be trained on me. I know I'm a dupe, a setup, a mark. I suppose I could take some solace in at least knowing ahead of time that I'll be laughed at and ridiculed instead of feeling ambushed when it happens.

As I drive past La-De-SPA, I'm surprised to see Calista's

car still parked in the small lot. It's after nine o'clock. Maybe she lives in an apartment above the spa? I realize I don't know much about her, despite the fact that I've spent the past two days in her salon. Armand found Calista's place by searching on the internet. Apparently he grilled her by phone to make sure she'd suffice, and then charmed her into closing the spa for two days to take care of me in privacy.

Calista has clearly thought of Armand, not me, as her client. She's talked as if she's known him for twenty years, while treating me like a perfect stranger. She has discussed personal aspects of my hair, skin, and nails with him while I've been sitting right there. Armand has made all the decisions, though he pretended to care about my opinion and repeatedly said I could overrule him. I never tried. I trust his taste in my camera-ready appearance far more than my own.

Calista put me in front of a webcam about thirty times for Armand's inspection. It has been humiliating, but Armand promises it will all be worth it when I wow the audience by looking "too fabulous to hate." It's good to know that I'm physically ready for tomorrow's interview, anyway.

While at the spa this morning, I saw a tabloid article with the headline: *What will Gwendolyn do next?* I was tempted to pick it up to see if any of their guesses struck a chord. Since coming back to Riveredge, I have lived a stopgap, emergency-mode life. I haven't given much thought to the future. There was a photo of me and Walter Owens standing in my driveway, unloading groceries from the trunk of his car. The caption was STOCKING THE LOVE NEST.

It doesn't seem to matter whether or not something is true, but whether consumers want it. I suppose I shouldn't really be surprised by that.

I had asked a maid I befriended at Walter's hotel if I could hire her to pick up some groceries for me. Walter must have caught wind of it, because instead of Sally coming by with my list, Walter showed up with a trunk full of things—most of which I didn't need or want—that he'd shopped for himself. While we unloaded his trunk, Walter asked me out yet again.

Yet again I said "no thanks." He had smiled like it was a strong maybe, but really it was another no thanks.

I wonder if Smith saw the stupid picture and believed the story; I wonder if he would care. I haven't spoken with Smith since I agreed to do the interview. I assume he's learned that it's going to happen. It would be hard not to know. I don't think he's aware that the reason I'm doing it is to clear away the mess I made him—that's a secret I've kept so he doesn't try to talk me out of it. I have attempted to call him a few times, and he has tried me, but we haven't connected. I guess that's the story of our lives.

Smith's house is on the route to my dad's. It's a beautiful place. With the outside lighting sort of blurred by the rain, I can imagine it as a painting. I like all the planes and cantilevers, and the enormous cedar front door, and the owner.

I can't help wishing that I'd gone into the master bedroom with him when I toured his house. I couldn't tell if he was flirting or teasing; it has always been too hard for me to know what Smith thinks. I wish I had just gone in and found out, or asked him how he felt, instead of trying to decipher him. If he wasn't going to be direct, I should have been.

If I thought he was home now, I'd be tempted to pull into his driveway and knock on the enormous front door. This is the hospital fundraiser evening, though. He's flashing his charming green eyes at a woman named Irene tonight.

I stop in the middle of the road in front of the Riveredge on Main and wait while some jaywalkers cross the wet and slushy street to Coach's Bar. They wave from under their umbrellas when they get close to the other curb and I wave back before heading on. I see there are many lights on in Walter's hotel, and though I cringe at the huge sign advertising the new Gwendolyn Golden Suite in all its lavender glory, I'm glad he seems to be doing brisk business. I'm not opening the door if he ever comes to my house again, though.

I pass by the hardware store and silently recite the list of things I need to get for the house: felt stickers for the bottoms of chairs, picture hangers, and a bigger doormat for the mud room.

Life has become more comfortable over the course of the week since I generated the confidence to take a utility knife to the boxes in the garage. All the things Caroline helped me order have arrived, and I managed to get most of them unpacked and set up. It's not perfect by any stretch. I know most of the screws could be a bit tighter, and I scratched the floor moving the sofa, and dented the kitchen table when I tried to set it up on its legs. The house is slowly becoming a home, though. An imperfect one, which suits me fine.

Megan's kids helped me with the smaller items when I babysat them Wednesday evening. Megan assured me she was only allowing me to do it because their regular sitter was sick, and Megan had cancelled a late meeting for the dinner date. She had on a soft gray wool dress and high black patent boots when she dropped the kids off. She said the house looked, "a little less hideous," and I could have said the same for her. Kyle waited in the car then, but he came in when they picked up the kids. He carried the sleeping children out to the car, one at a time.

I sent Caroline a thank you basket of goodies for helping me buy all my stuff for the house. Armand told me where to send it from. She called and offered to come by with a paint deck to help me choose colors for the walls. I told her that I hung several canvases already, and it's looking brighter and happier, but I'd absolutely love her advice. We set a date for next weekend, when her kids will be with her husband who just moved back to town.

I was surprised that Caroline would choose to hang out with me on her first night of freedom, but I'm looking forward to it. Armand sent me a simple pasta with dried cherries and fancy cheeses recipe to try, and told me which wine would go. I feel safe attempting to cook for Caroline. I don't think she'll judge me if I fail.

I guess I'm getting pretty cozy here in Riveredge. My hometown is starting to feel like home.

I didn't have to think twice when Armand's agent offered me representation. I have no interest whatsoever in the media any more. It's like a pie eating contest winner being offered the chance to be a pie taster—as if she could possibly appreciate pie after making herself profoundly sick from too much of it.

I punch the code into the entry gate and drive slowly into my dad's senior community. I pull into his driveway just behind Megan.

"You're here, too? He's okay, isn't he?" I ask.

"I think so. He said he needed to talk to the two of us." She hugs her coat tighter around her, looking as confused as I feel.

I'd ask her how it's going at home, but I fear she'd bite my head off and say it's not my business. My dad stares out the front door, watching us walk up.

Inside, he directs us to the dining area and points to the round wooden table that used to sit in the breakfast nook when we were children. He takes three beers out of the fridge and opens them. I almost tell him no thanks, but I don't think he would hear me. His expression is focused on something far away. Megan and I exchange concerned glances and sit down.

My dad takes a long drink of his beer and I see that his hands are shaking. The only other time I remember his hands shaking was at my mother's funeral. He sits down and looks at each of us for a long moment, as if gathering his will.

"I have to tell you girls something."

He looks nervous and uncomfortable, and I want to reassure him. When I reach out to touch his hand, he wards me off.

"Come on. It can't be that bad," I say, but I'm nervous.

My dad takes another long drink of his beer and then sets it aside. He puts his hands together and looks down at them resting on the table.

"Your mom was a difficult woman in many ways, but I always admired her. It was hardest when she became sick. I thought she'd make it through because she was always such a fighter."

Megan sniffs and takes a sip of her beer. She has no patience with the topic of our mother since her death. I don't think she ever forgave her for dying unexpectedly during a surgery that everyone was sure would come out just fine. I had only been sad, but Megan had been angry.

"Only a few weeks before she died, your mom did something that she was very sorry about. I want to tell you right here and now, and I want you to remember: *I* helped her cover it up. So I am just as guilty as your mom was." My dad says this defiantly, like he knows we're going to argue.

We don't though. We wait tensely, wondering what this is about.

"It was late, and I don't even remember why she was out by herself. It was Poker night, and the guys were at our house. She came home white as a mummy and they all took off, making excuses left and right. Sometimes it pained me that no one seemed to like your mom. When the men had gone, she showed me her Suburban parked in the garage. It had a smashed bumper, and there was a lot of blood."

I feel my stomach drop out, like I'm falling from a terrible height, and there's nothing to catch me.

"She said she wasn't sure what she'd hit. Thought it might've been a deer, they were so thick that year, and Sharon Pasternak had totaled her car hitting one just a few nights before. But I think your mom knew it was a person, somewhere deep down, because she just kept getting whiter."

I feel Megan's hand go over mine, but it doesn't really register consciously. Everything has receded from my mind except my dad's face, and his voice, and his hand shaking around his bottle of beer.

"I drove my car to town and saw the ambulance. I kept driving past. Whoever it was, they were getting help. I had your mom to worry about. I went back home to her, but I could already tell it was the beginning of the end. She sort of lost her fight all at once. I think your mom was ninety percent fight, so there wasn't much left to her without it."

"Did Smith know it was Mom who hit him?" Megan asks in a whisper.

I turn to look at her and I know her face mirrors mine. She looks horrified, as one can only be at a grave and undeniable truth, not an idea or a question.

My dad nods solemnly.

"And he didn't tell anyone?" Megan asks, like she can't quite absorb this piece of information. "*Why* didn't he tell anyone?"

"I went to his hospital room when he was still in critical condition. He was a mess, but he knew why I was there before I said anything. He sent everyone else out. I told him that Emma was sorry. So sorry. He said he knew that must be true. I asked if he could see it in his heart to not press charges against her, and explained about her stomach cancer and her surgery coming up. I promised him Emma wouldn't drive again."

The three of us sit in silence for a while, not looking at each other.

"I sold the Suburban to an auction company in Ohio."

I feel empty. Sad. Sick. I wish there was someone to be mad at, a clear evil person who did a horrible thing and could be punished now. A chance at justice. I feel as powerless as my dad looks as he finishes his beer with a trembling hand.

"When Emma died, Smith Walker sent flowers. He was still in the hospital."

"He just let her get away with it?" Megan asks. She grips my hand hard and it hurts.

"I guess he didn't see a point in ruining the rest of her life."

"What about the rest of *his* life?" Megan demands.

"Dad was just trying to help his wife," I tell my sister as I pull my hand away. I touch her shoulder softly. I don't want her to yell anymore.

Megan looks at me like she might argue. Her expression shifts from anger to sad acceptance and she puts her head down on the table.

"Why did you tell us now, Dad?" I ask.

"I was afraid it would come out in the interview tomorrow. Before your interview here, that reporter asked questions like she knew the truth already. I've been trying to bring it up ever since, but I couldn't work up the nerve."

He looks sorrowful, like he's afraid I'll stop loving him right here and right now, reversing a lifetime of habit. I lean over and hug him for a long time. When I get up, I push my untouched beer in front of him.

"I'm heading out," I tell them both, taking keys out of my pocket.

"I know Smith kept quiet for you, Gwenny. He liked you so much," my dad says.

"He still does." Megan lifts her head to look at me. "He loves you. Broken down, loyal Smith Walker loves you more than handsome, cheating Kyle has *ever* loved me." She looks away again. "I would trade in a heartbeat."

The sky has been overcast and gray all day, threatening rain for hours on end, then drizzling for only ten minutes or so before brooding again. I got used to sunshine in North Carolina, along with the good painting light it provided. Sometimes a sunny day would cloud up, and there would be a rain shower, sometimes an angry one, but the sun generally came back out again soon afterward. If weather were a personality, North Carolina would be generally happy but occasionally have a little tantrum from which it recovered quickly. It had cloudy stretches of course, like little bouts of the humdrums, but nothing like Michigan, which can be dreary for days and days until you forget the sun even exists. Today Michigan has pouted and sniffled, but instead of simply having a fit and getting it over with, it has been brewing.

As I pull into Smith's driveway and shut off my car, I hear, see, and feel the sky open up. I don't have an umbrella with me, but I get out and walk with my head down toward the front door.

I have to talk to him, to see him.

I haven't thought this through… I don't know what I'll say. I want to tell him that I know what happened. That I know what a brave, chivalrous, and unselfish man he is, and has always been. Maybe I won't say anything at all, just fall into his arms and never let go. I slide on a slushy patch of black asphalt and catch myself. The rain is freezing as it hits my face.

Almost to the door, I look into a window. I see past the foyer into the lamp lit family room. I stop, like a hungry beggar outside a house of plenty on Christmas Eve.

I see Smith sitting on the built-in sofa, close to a pretty

blonde woman with a heart-shaped face. She's laughing at something he said. They're drinking red wine, and the flames from the fireplace make the scene glow. Though it had been heavy on my mind before going to my dad's, I had forgotten about Smith's date tonight. The woman, Irene, touches his hand and looks into his kind green eyes.

My feet are numb in my boots as I turn and stumble back to the car.

chapter twenty-two

armand

"How does it feel to be back in the *So Perfect* house?" Stuart Bolder asks with a huge smile. I saw his makeup girl penciling his dimples, and the way she worked on his black eye, I think maybe he'll have it six months from now if it still helps his ratings. He wears *way* too much makeup in general. I like a man to look more like a man.

Stuart is sitting beside me on the same gorgeous, distressed leather sofa with the fabulous tufts and rolled arms where we sat together three weeks ago. It's on a platform again, facing our dining room live audience of fifty. I have some ideas about how we can cram some more adoring fans in here and disrupt the living spaces less, but I have to recheck my measurements before I roll the plans out to Trey and Stuart like a little red carpet.

I have so many ideas! And for once, I'll actually have the power to make them happen.

Gwendolyn is on the far side of Stuart. I wish she was sitting beside me so I could nudge her awake. She's staring down at her hands like she didn't hear the question, which was clearly directed to her. She's playing hard to get, but I know we can break through that.

I clear my throat and take charge of the situation. "There's actually no place I'd rather be. This house has always felt like home to me, from the moment I first saw her. She was looking somewhat shabby then, I admit, but she sure cleaned up nice," I say, smiling big, but not too big. I don't want my gums to show.

"Are you talking about this house or Gwendolyn?" Stuart

leans over to her, like they're old friends sharing a laugh. Maybe he thinks they are, in a weird way.

"You look like you've gotten all fixed up for tonight's interview. I barely recognized you from the last time I saw you," Stuart says.

She ignores him. That's better than what I feared, which was an elbow to the chin. The tension here is so high I wish I'd had me some of the devil to calm my nerves before I sat down. I bite my lip and pick at the faded remains of turquoise paint on the sofa arm.

"Cut for a second," Stuart tells the cameraman. He turns to Trey and throws up his hands in frustration. "Want to see if you can wake up Ms. Golden so she can join our little party here?"

The audience starts talking among themselves while Trey comes over and speaks to Gwendolyn in a low whisper. "Our agreement is that you have to *participate* in this interview. If you don't hold up your end of the bargain, all bets are off."

She glares at him. "Fine, you dickhead."

"Oh, that's nice. We give you a chance to come back to center stage and you act like we're villains? Don't worry, Ms. Golden, this is the last time we'll invite you to this house. Right, Armand?"

I shush him and shoo him away in a flurry as I kneel down by Gwendolyn's side. I look up into her face and adjust a few strands of tamed hair, silently thanking Calista for doing in two days what should have taken as many weeks.

"What did Trey mean by that?" she asks.

"Oh, nothing," I lie.

I wish I'd had more time with Gwendolyn before the taping began, but her plane was late, and by the time she was ready I'd had to get my mama all situated, which wasn't easy. My mother didn't want to sit on "no cold metal bench," so I'd had to haul in one of the tapestry wing chairs from the library. She doesn't exactly blend well with the forty-nine other audience members, and looking out at her gives me an image of how she'd look in her tent dress and comfy walking shoes beside me in my Speedo in the French Riviera, where she's been hinting she'd like to go.

It ain't ever happening, I tell myself, and wonder if it's true because I wouldn't have believed this would happen either. Yet somehow she's fifteen feet away, perched high above everybody else, like an unhappy judge getting ready to lay down the law but good.

I turn to focus on Gwendolyn, and how I can save this interview. I don't have time to explain the whole situation now. I should have explained it earlier, but she'll know soon enough what's going on. And I know she'll be happy for me!

"You look gorgeous," I say, fixing the necklace she somehow managed to put on wrong. I wipe at a smudge on one of the shoes she's only had on her feet for twenty minutes, because I knew she'd mess up the shiny patent leather if I gave them to her any earlier. "More beautiful than ever!" I smile.

Gwendolyn doesn't.

"Come on now kid, work with me here! Please?" I beg.

She rolls her eyes. But finally, finally, finally she nods yes.

I get up and rush to my seat when I'm told. I don't want to screw anything up! I blow a kiss to my Jens who came again to see me on my big day. I see Carl has added lowlights to their hair. They give me a loud cheer that boosts my spirits as I sit down.

The interview starts up again.

"The audience wants to know all about the shiner I got the last time I saw you," he points to his eye as if anyone could possibly miss it. "I wouldn't have guessed that little Riveredge, Michigan could be so dangerous."

"Yes, you got a black eye," Gwendolyn says, like a hostile witness.

"How have you been spending your time since your friend beat me up?"

She looks out to the audience. Most of the people seated on the long, metal benches seem really interested in how she'll answer, like she's an old friend who has been away a while, and they've been wondering how she's been. Her expression gets softer and she talks right to them, ignoring Stuart completely.

"I've spent a lot of time with my father. He has downsized to a condo in a senior community where he plays poker and shoots pool. I've enjoyed getting to know him again; I had been gone for a long time. Over the past week I've gotten more settled into my new house. And I've been painting quite a lot."

"So you really do paint? That part was real?" Stuart asks.

That was a terrible thing for Stuart to say and I'd like to tell him so! But the unfortunate truth is that I've never been very good at telling off someone in a position of power over me.

Gwendolyn glares at Stuart and becomes hostile again. "Yes."

"How have you been spending your time, Armand?" Stuart asks, turning to me.

I look at my mother sitting above the other audience members, like they may be the jury, but she'll overrule anything she darn well wants to, honey.

I chuckle to try and build up some confidence. I remind myself how good I look in this sweater, and these fabulous new jeans. I know my face is red though, and my voice comes out shaky. "Well, you know, a little of this, a little of that."

"And some of it on television, right?"

"As much as possible," I agree. My Jens give another cheer and my smile widens.

Stuart lowers his voice, as if this conversation is nothing but friendly and easygoing, as if it's not being filmed and he's not going to edit it.

"There has been a lot of speculation about your love life, Armand. Are you dating anyone now?"

Keeping my smile hoisted up is too hard. I let it fall. "No I'm not, Stuart. Thanks for asking."

"What about you, Gwendolyn? You've been photographed with your hometown hotel manager Walter Owens, *and* the man some tabloids have uncharitably referred to as Scar Face, but who I like to call Right Hook." Stuart motions a punch and points to his black eye. "Are you dating either of them?"

Gwendolyn looks out at the audience with a slight smile, pretending she didn't hear the question. She checks her watch.

Stuart calls for another break in the taping and beelines it over to Trey Hammond and Josie. The three of them put their heads together and talk quickly.

I slide into Stuart's empty seat.

"What?" Gwendolyn asks, real bitchy-like. "Is my hair out of place? Is there a wrinkle in my skirt or another scuff on my shoe that you can't quite live with, even though you're always saying that you love the Grand Dame *for* her imperfections? Do you want to fight over this stupid aquamarine paint on the sofa?" She points to another smudge I hadn't noticed yet and I wince. "How exactly am I screwing everything up this time? I know you're dying to tell me."

"You hate me?" I ask.

Gwendolyn frowns and I worry that if she makes a habit of it she'll get all wrinkled up. I know better than to mention it right this minute, though.

"I'm just so damn sick of going along with other people's ideas, and believing other people's take on what's good or bad about me, and for me. That's what landed me here in the first place," she says.

Stuart wedges between us as the camera light goes back on.

"It looks like you'll have to be the life of this party, Armand," he says.

That's our cue. I reply just like we planned. "That's no problem!" I say, flashing a big smile. I peek over at Josie on the sideline to make sure I did it right, like a child star to a stage mom. This is my big moment, when I get to announce my new show to the world. I try to pump myself up for it.

Gwendolyn's got me all confused, though, and I feel like I'm full of holes now, with air whooshing out of me, making me flatter by the second. It's the same way I felt that afternoon when I was ten and came home from school early to find Reverend Sugarbaker sitting at the kitchen table in my mama's bathrobe.

Stuart isn't waiting for me to catch up. He's going full steam ahead with our plan.

"Tonight we have a big surprise in store. You all remember Armand and Gwendolyn's journey here with *So Perfect*, don't you? For those of you who may have missed it, let's watch the transformation these two have undergone, from their very first catalog, until now."

The red Chinese doors over the flat screen TV pull back for the studio audience to watch a three minute history. There are more monitors around the room, we placed them just so. I divide my attention between the nearest screen, my glowering mama, and Gwendolyn, who's staring at her pumps. I want to tell her what's about to happen but there isn't time. I should have told her before, I know I should have.

Four years of me and Gwendolyn, our hair and clothing styles, and our growing coziness with each other are shown on the video. It makes me choke up to see the way we were. I'm scared that I broke us by thinking of me, me, and me again, leaving the poor kid in the dust.

Harsher music starts up and the scandal is rehashed, beginning with the photo of Norman and me that started it all, followed by a photo of Gwendolyn driving out in tears in that ugly beige t-shirt. I cover my eyes to miss the footage of me laughing about the poor kid's household helplessness. The trip down memory lane ends at Gwendolyn's stark and empty new house.

Stuart stands and motions for a close up on me.

"How do fans of *So Perfect* want this story to end?" he asks, looking at the audience, then into the camera. It's obvious that he's rehearsed these lines in front of a mirror at least a gazillion times, and he would've been way better off winging it. After he pauses for so long, and stares all weird like he thinks he's his own drumroll machine, he says:

"They don't want it to end!"

The audience cheers.

I rehearsed my response too, but I don't want to do it the way I thought I did. I don't want to be the only phoenix rising up out of these ashes.

Gwendolyn crosses her arms and frowns at me.

Stuart beams like a proud father. "Tonight we're announcing that Armand is going to have his own syndicated show, produced by our very own WJKS."

The Jens stand up and shout. I wave to them for a second,

but my hand feels heavy. I watch the confetti drop from the ceiling as planned. I peek over to see Gwendolyn looking frustrated, like she's been waiting seven hours to take a driving test at the DMV.

"Are you excited, Armand?" Stuart asks.

"Yes!" I say as happily as I can.

I toss my arm around Gwendolyn's shoulder to try and show we're still a team. And the truth is, the best times I've ever had were right here in this house, with Gwendolyn by my side. I realize that I don't want to do this without her. As the idea gels in my mind, I just announce it, loud and proud.

"And I want Gwendolyn to be right here with me. What do you say, kid?"

"No."

She answers so quietly I have to ask twice. My arm is still around her, though I feel her shoulders go rigid and I'm afraid to look at her.

"Did you say no?" Stuart asks.

The audience boos a little, especially those with new lowlights.

"No," Gwendolyn repeats.

I sneak a peek at her face and she looks like the long wait at the DMV has officially pissed her off.

"Listen," I say right to her, pretending that we're alone, wishing we were. "We won't have to pretend anything. You can escape depressing old Riveredge, move back in here, and we'll live together again in this beautiful house. I'll cook for you, Alejandra and Miguel will come back, and it'll be just like old times. It'll even better, because we won't have to pretend anymore!"

She looks at me, then out to my mama in the audience, then at me again. My smile falls away.

"You're the real star," Gwendolyn tells me as she reaches out and takes my hand in both of hers. She looks to the audience and raises her voice. "Right? Armand can do it without me! I'm not much fun without a script anyway. I mean, how many times can you watch someone light a kitchen on fire?" She puts her arm around my waist, like she's a life ring and she doesn't want me to sink after all.

"But we'd have fun. It would be real this time," I beg. I realize I want her here with me more than anything.

She shakes her head. "No. I can't do it. There is nothing real about this for me, Armand. There never has been, except you, and the other good people I've met. I love you. But I don't want this. I won't do it."

"You could paint all day. We'd have so much fun! Maybe bring on guests, and throw parties! What could be more real?" I ask.

"Family. Home. Love." She counts them off on her fingers.

Stuart perks up. "Are you saying you're prepared to give up Armand's generous offer to let you ride on his coattails for your 'as is' *home* in Michigan, your *family* that's so small they can all fit inside it, and for *love*? You mean you actually love Walter Owens, the hotel manager?"

"No."

"Don't tell me you're in love with Scar Face!"

Gwendolyn looks out to the audience. The room becomes perfectly silent and everyone seems to be holding their breath, including me. Finally she smiles warmly and turns to Stuart.

"Yes, actually. Thanks for asking, because I wasn't sure how I was going to say it on my own. I do love Smith Walker."

She puts her hand under my chin and I look into her eyes, made so pretty and soft by her expression. "I love Smith Walker," she says.

I smile because I've never seen her look so happy, or so strong.

She looks out to the audience. "I love Smith Walker." She looks into the camera. "I hope they don't edit this part out, Smith Walker, because I want you to know once and for all: I love you."

"You've got to be kidding me!" Stuart says, shaking his head like someone just threw up on his shoes.

"Am I done here?" Gwendolyn stands and looks at Trey. "Are we finished? Does this fulfill my part of our agreement?"

He confers briefly with Stuart. Then he nods.

She removes her microphone and walks down the steps from the makeshift stage.

I watch her go.

"Well that's a surprise, isn't it? Your unexpected and overly generous offer was turned down. You've been passed over, Armand," Stuart says, shaking his head like he's never seen anything so crazy.

"Shut the hell up," I say, putting my head into my hands and leaning over to rest my elbows on my knees. I need to collect myself.

When I sit back up, I look straight out to the judge in the audience.

"Ma'am, I am a gay man," I say.

My mama glares at me until I break my gaze.

I look out over the audience and take a deep breath. I smile so wide, maybe my gums are showing, but I don't care right now.

"Everyone, I'm a gay man!"

My Jens jump to their feet and applaud, bless their hearts.

"Wait for me, Gwendolyn!" I call as I strip off my microphone and run after her.

chapter twenty-three

caroline

Armand is sentimental and nostalgic, and I don't blame him a bit. It has been three months since his last interview in this house, and he's been counting down to today with growing excitement.

"There were years that I had expected to be a big deal," he says. "Like turning sixteen meant I could drive a car, eighteen meant I was officially and legally a grown up, twenty-one meant I could throw away my fake ID, and thirty meant I wasn't in my twenties anymore."

He looks to me and I smile. He drinks in approval like a sweet but kicked around dog, like a child who's had way too much criticism and not nearly enough praise.

"You know Caroline, I just never expected that thirty-one would be so damn transformative. But here I am! And I may as well start the clock over, honey. I feel born again, like my life is just starting."

"I know what you mean. But we have exactly one hour before the audience files in to their seats, so you'd better go get dressed!"

Armand tried to tell me what to wear today, but I reminded him that I'm not Gwendolyn. I let him choose between the two outfits the wardrobe woman helped me pick, but slapped his hands away when he tried to adjust my bra.

"I'm gay!" he said.

"So? Hands off."

"I hope you're not such a prude with that handsome husband of yours."

"Seriously, I should sue you for harassment!" I said, and he made catlike movements and hissed.

"Takes one to know one."

When Armand asked me to work on his show, I said no at first. After I thought about it for a while and talked it over with Gwendolyn, I called him back. Armand and I went through some pretty heated negotiations until we were both comfortable.

In order to keep life stable for my kids, I'll film my little pieces at WJKS's sister station in Michigan. Occasionally I'll fly in for special occasions, like today's taping, but it wouldn't really fit my position to gallivant excessively even if I wanted to. One of my roles on the show is to be the Cost Conscience.

The idea came up when Armand told me about his idea for a travel feature, which would consist of him going somewhere fabulous, with cameras following him around. He thought Venice first, then maybe Monaco, then Paris...

I didn't mention the fact that his idea sounded pointless. Instead I asked if he had any idea about the recession we're in. I suggested that a budget-minded travel segment might be nice. The show could send a family somewhere interesting within minivan driving distance of their home, and help them find ways to entertain themselves and dine inexpensively. Blake helped me demonstrate the idea here in Scenic. He and the kids have been touring museums, taking walking tours, fishing, and playing on the beach. They won't be able to fit in all the things on their list before we head back home to Riveredge again.

Riveredge, Michigan is a great place to collect cost saving ideas. My Cost Conscience segments will reflect the reality that so many people are facing as they try to make it in an expensive world with less money than they used to have. Armand supported the idea wholeheartedly, though I'm sure he's glad I'll do the segments instead of him. He's ready to live large, and I'm not going to try to make him feel guilty about it. He has already experienced enough guilt for one lifetime.

Armand also dubbed me the show's Mother Superior. He has a penchant for religious naming conventions, but I'm picking my battles and letting my silly titles slide for now. I'm glad I'll be able to do occasional kid-oriented cooking, crafting, and decorating reports from Michigan. I've got plenty of room since we bought the old house back from Gwendolyn. Blake lives there now but leaves me space to work. He has been helping with the kids so that I have time to do all the legwork, promotion, and taping required for my small role on Armand's show.

Blake has continued to insist that he never had an affair with Francine. I told him about Kyle and I guess we're forgiving each other a little at a time. I don't know what's going to happen. The biggest thing I've learned over the course of this year is that life is one big surprise after another, and maybe I should loosen up and try my best to roll with it.

Armand struggled to find the right name for his show. He was cleared to use *So Perfect* if he wanted. The name recognition was certainly there, but he said it just didn't feel right to him anymore. He knew what he didn't want, but of all the new names he tried on, none seemed to fit.

I accidentally stumbled upon one. We'd been brainstorming segment ideas when I suggested doing one on foreclosed houses, explaining the potential money saving benefits along with the dangers. I said, "You have to understand what you're getting, because you're buying *as is*."

He put up his hand to stop me and tried out the words: *AS IS*.

He said they called to him. He thought they could go right up on a banner and become a motto for acceptance. Not an excuse to settle necessarily, but a reminder that at a certain point, you just need to say, *OK, enough is enough! I'm sick of chasing the dream of perfection and that's not a failure.* Whether that means finally learning to smile at yourself in the mirror, living happily with your old car for a few more years, or in Armand's case, "holding your head high when your mama says you needn't ever call her again."

AS IS made sense to me, too. It might be like a pop song that everyone finds a different meaning inside, singing along as if it was written especially for you. Armand called Gwendolyn on speakerphone right away to run the idea by her and she loved it. She actually said, "It's so perfect!"

chapter twenty-four

smith

It's one of those Michigan days that make you breathe easy. The sun shines and the sky is a hopeful hue, full of promise. The few clouds that billow past aren't there to block out the sun, but to provide a counterpoint to the brilliant blue.

The clouds are the picture kind. I see a woman's long, lean profile lounging within one. I see a house with a chimney billowing friendly smoke plumes that are made up of other clouds. I see a fat, healthy baby. I stop cloud-watching when Taylor reaches out and touches my elbow. I look up and catch my breath.

I used to think that if a moment in my life were ever truly perfect, I could say, *Okay, that's it, that's all I needed and I can die now. If this is my time, I won't argue.* But that was bullshit.

Gwen waves from far up the path, holding on to her dad's arm. Her white satin dress moves in the slight breeze. She looks like an angel.

She smiles at me. There has never been a moment in my life quite like this one, and I know that if my number was called right now, I'd put up one hell of a fight.

She wanted the wedding here at Riveredge Park. It has always been a special place to us, though we didn't come here all that often, each time was meaningful somehow. Our invitation had the picture she'd drawn of us here on the back, a contemporary photograph of us here on the cover. The words: *A celebration of love* formed a simple frame.

Everything about today is simple. We kept the guest list

small and I called on a few of my connections to keep this section of the park free from curiosity seekers or reporters.

My family takes up most of the seats. Siler and Janet and their sons sit with my mom and her boyfriend Caleb in the front row. My other brothers and their wives sit in the next row, and several cousins fill in behind. Jessie and Jack brought Jessie's mother Pinky along, and the ancient lady's indelicate snoring is like a dueling banjo against Armand's sobs across the aisle. He sits close to Caroline Penny and her family like he belongs with them. Irene holds hands in the back row with a marathoner she's been bragging about the past few Friday mornings. I'm happy for her. I'm happy for all of us

Gwen's niece Leah and my lispy niece Crane share the flower girl honors. Taylor stands sturdily beside me. Megan marched up ahead of Gwen, crying as if they've always been best friends, though last night they insulted each other and I bet they will at the reception as well.

Gordy Golden gives me a solemn nod as he and Gwen reach the place where I stand waiting. I offer her my free arm. As she takes hold, I feel the coolness of her silk glove on my hand.

She leans in close and whispers, "I wished for you."

I think of all the years, and pain, and regret, and longing, and healing since I last heard Gwen say those words to me. I have to stop for a moment to collect myself. My emotions run closer to the surface since the accident, as I may have already mentioned.

I have to take my hand away from Gwen to reach for a handkerchief in my pocket. I wipe my eyes. She waits. Everyone waits. I'm not mortified by embarrassment, I'm simply living this moment, the best of my life so far. It fills me up; I have no time or room for anything else.

When I'm able, I look at Gwen. She smiles and I smile back, and we take a tighter hold of each other. Together we turn to face the minister standing in front of a gnarled old oak.

acknowledgments

Thanks to Joe Veltre and Alice Lawson from the Gersh Agency for believing in my work and finding me a comfortable home at Diversion Books. I will always be grateful.

Thanks to Randall Klein—a funny, perceptive, and wise editor—and the rest of the excellent Diversion Books team.

Thanks to Mary Jane and Bob Michael, my amazing parents. As the ninth of ten children, I'd like to particularly thank them for being such good Catholics. They raised us with laughter, and allowed each of us to be who we are.

Thanks to Abby, Abe, and Anna for cracking me up, trying my patience, and making life an adventure. They are loved beyond measure.

Thanks to Paul, for everything.